PUFFIN

Ghost Detectives

THE LOST BRIDE

Ghost Detectives

THE LOST BRIDE

Emily Mason

PUFFIN

PUFFIN BOOKS

Published by the Penguin Group
Penguin Books Ltd, 80 Strand, London WC2R ORL, England
Penguin Group (USA) Inc., 375 Hudson Street, New York, New York 10014, USA
Penguin Group (Canada), 90 Eglinton Avenue East, Suite 700, Toronto, Ontario, Canada M4P 2Y3
(a division of Pearson Penguin Canada Inc.)
Penguin Ireland, 25 St Stephen's Green, Dublin 2, Ireland (a division of Penguin Books Ltd)
Penguin Group (Australia), 250 Camberwell Road, Camberwell, Victoria 3124, Australia
(a division of Pearson Australia Group Pty Ltd)
Penguin Books India Pvt Ltd, 11 Community Centre, Panchsheel Park, New Delhi – 110 017, India
Penguin Group (NZ), 67 Apollo Drive, Rosedale, Auckland 0632, New Zealand
(a division of Pearson New Zealand Ltd)
Penguin Books (South Africa) (Pty) Ltd, Block D, Rosebank Office Park,
181 Jan Smuts Avenue, Parktown North, Gauteng 2193, South Africa

Penguin Books Ltd, Registered Offices: 80 Strand, London WC2R ORL, England

puffinbooks.com

First published 2012
001 – 10 9 8 7 6 5 4 3 2 1

Text copyright © Rachel Pierce, 2012
All rights reserved

The moral right of the author and illustrator has been asserted

Set in 13/16pt Baskerville By Palimpsest Book Production Limited,
Falkirk, Stirlingshire
Printed in Great Britain by Clays Ltd, St Ives plc

British Library Cataloguing in Publication Data
A CIP catalogue record for this book is available from the British Library

ISBN: 978-0-141-34202-3

www.greenpenguin.co.uk

ALWAYS LEARNING   **PEARSON**

For Breeda and Nicholas, of course

Contents

I

The List

Abigail Worthy was standing in the corridor, chewing on the end of a pencil and staring at a piece of paper pinned to the wall. She glanced around, as if she was afraid someone might catch her there. She looked at the paper again: sign or don't sign? The list was only half full, so she could do it, but would her new schoolmates think she was uncool for wanting to do it? At home in her old school, back in Massachusetts, she would have put her name down without a second thought. Her friends there would have been into the idea and they would have joined together. But here she hadn't figured out yet how things worked. She'd only moved to the town that summer, after her mom got a new job she'd always wanted, and school had only started that week. It wasn't enough time to know what these kids thought about anything.

One of the young teachers, Miss Flood, was looking for ten volunteers to work Saturdays in the old town museum. Abi wasn't entirely sure what they'd have to do, but it sounded interesting, and she never had anything to do at the weekend because she hadn't made any friends yet. Two days was a long time when you saw no one but your own family.

Above the list it said:

Please put down your name if you are free on Saturdays and willing to spend about four hours working in the Grainger house, the site of the former town museum. The project will involve organizing the house and its contents with a view to re-opening it as a public museum in the near future. It will be hard work, but an unforgettable experience!

So far, four people had put their names down: Josh Fitzsimons, Daniel Binoche, Jack Bateman, Solomon Uba – all boys. Abi went back to chewing her pencil, wondering who they were and what they might be like. Friendly or not, she supposed, she'd at least get to know them if they were working together, and they might even be fun to hang out with.

All right, she thought, *I'm going to do it.* She scribbled her name quickly on the list so she couldn't change her mind again. As she was opening her bag to drop her well-bitten pencil into it, the door behind her banged open, making her jump.

'Sorry about that,' a voice called out cheerfully.

Abi turned round to see three girls coming towards her. The door crasher was a girl she'd seen around – well, you couldn't miss her. She stood out from the rest with her customized uniform, crazy hairstyles and pink Converse. Today, she had a stripy belt round her waist, a line of bracelets on her wrist and red knee socks, which should have looked strange against the hot pink of her trainers, but somehow she made it look great. Her hair was in a network of plaits and she had the sort of cheeky smile that made Abi immediately start smiling too.

'Are you putting your name down for the Grainger thing?' the girl asked.

Uh-oh, moment of truth – were they going to tease her for doing it? 'Well, yeah, I thought I might,' Abi said quietly.

'Me too!' said the girl, smiling even wider. 'I'm Grace. And my friends Hannah and Sarah are going to do it as well. This is Hannah,' she said, pointing at the girl with long, straight blonde hair to die for. Abigail had had plenty of time to envy that hair because Hannah sat a few rows up from her in class. 'She's a total nerd,' Grace said, nodding over at Hannah, 'so this is right up her street.'

'Hey,' said Hannah, giving Grace a friendly nudge. 'I just like history, that's all,' she said in a soft voice, smiling shyly at Abi.

Grace laughed and turned to the other girl who was with her. 'And this is Sarah.' Abi smiled at

Sarah, admiring her wavy red hair and green eyes. She'd noticed her in class before too – she'd love to have red hair herself, instead of normal brown hair in a boring pixie crop, with her large hazel eyes to match. She felt she looked so dorky next to these girls.

'Hi there,' Abi said. The three girls seemed really friendly, if different as chalk and cheese – she couldn't imagine how they'd all become friends. But, if they were doing the project too, it might just be a bit of fun after all.

Grace took a pen from her pocket and began to fill in her own name and her friends' names on the list, her bracelets jangling as she wrote.

'Where are you from?' Sarah said, her wide green eyes looking curiously at Abi, like Abi was some weird animal in the zoo.

Hannah rolled her eyes. 'Always so polite, Sarah,' she murmured.

'Don't mind Sarah,' Grace said over her shoulder, writing the last name on the list with a flourish. 'She's very straight to the point!'

'I was only asking!' Sarah said, laughing.

'I don't mind,' Abi said with a grin. 'I'm from America. Springfield, Massachusetts. I moved here during the summer.'

'Springfield?' Hannah said. 'Isn't that where –'

'The Simpsons!' Grace interrupted. 'Yeah, it's where the Simpsons live.'

4

Hannah shook her head. 'I was going to say that it's where Dr Seuss is from. You know, the place he writes about in his very famous book about Mulberry Street?' She turned to Abi. 'I feel sorry for you, Abi, moving to a school like this, where people don't know their Simpsons from their Dr Seuss.'

Abi looked at them uncertainly until Grace winked at her, then poked Hannah in the ribs. 'Know-it-all,' she said. 'Just because you love books doesn't mean the rest of us have to.'

'Fashion victim,' Hannah shot back, making Grace screech.

'Losers,' Sarah said, making an L-shape on her forehead with her hand. They all burst out laughing and Abi looked around happily. After a week of strange faces and strange accents and no friends in sight, finally it seemed like she'd met some girls she could really get to like.

Suddenly Sarah stopped laughing and her face creased into a frown as she stared through the glass panels of the door behind them. 'Here comes trouble,' she muttered.

2

Chrissy and the Clones

'Well, I do have dressage on Saturday mornings, but it's at eight, so I'm sure I can fit in the museum work too,' Chrissy Edwards was saying in a loud voice as she came through the door with her friends. 'It sounds like the kind of project I could really shine at, you know, with my natural flair for –' She stopped short when she saw the four girls standing in front of the list.

'Hi,' she said in the same loud voice, with a very fake smile. 'Oh, Grace, I meant to say to you earlier, I just *love* how you're rocking the uniform today.' Behind her, her three friends started to snigger and Abi saw Grace blush. 'We're just signing up as volunteers,' Chrissy said, pointing at the list on the wall behind them.

'I would have thought working for free was beneath you, Chrissy,' Sarah said pointedly.

Abi saw Chrissy's friends tense up, anticipating a row. She'd seen them in the lunch hall on Monday, talking loudly about all the 'fabulous' things they'd

6

done that summer, and something about their loudness and self-importance had really put her off. She'd just known they weren't the kind of girls she'd get on with. Looking at them now, squaring up behind Chrissy, she knew she was right. The smallest one had blonde hair and was pretty, but she seemed to watch the others constantly and follow everything they did. Abi knew the tall girl's name was Sophie and that she narrowed her eyes in a way that made her look mean. The other one was standing close to Chrissy now, looking delighted at the idea of a showdown. *Freak*, Abi thought to herself. *How could anyone enjoy confrontations?*

Chrissy put a hand on her hip and pouted at Sarah. 'I'd actually see myself more as *directing* things, Sarah. I'm really good at seeing the big picture and knowing how to get things done. Now, if you'll excuse me . . .'

She took a step towards them, and Abi and the girls shuffled to the side to let her get to the list. She flicked back her glossy black curls and clicked her fingers at her friends. 'Pen,' she demanded, holding out her hand. The girl with blonde hair immediately rooted out a pen and passed it to her. 'Thanks, Tiffany,' Chrissy said sweetly.

Watching all this, Abi thought that Chrissy would have fitted in well at her old school, as one of the cool girls – the ones with shiny long hair and attitudes as sharp as needles. She looked exactly like the kind of girl who could make your life a misery, if she felt like it. She had gorgeous black hair that fell in loose curls on her shoulders, as if she'd had it done in a salon that morning. Her uniform was immaculate and she was wearing a slick of peach lip gloss, which was totally against school rules. It was obvious her friends thought she was the queen bee, and tried to look like her and talk like her. Abi felt her stomach tighten – she'd been teased by girls like this all through school. She had hoped it would be different here.

Chrissy raised the pen to the list, then sighed impatiently. 'There's only two places left,' she said.

'I don't mind not –' Tiffany began in a small voice.

Chrissy flashed her a look. 'No, we're *all* going to do it, Tiffany. It's not a problem.' Sophie tittered as Tiffany blushed, taking great satisfaction in hearing Chrissy silence her like that. 'I'll just add in your name and Sophie's,' Chrissy went on, 'and explain to Miss Flood that she needs girls like us involved.' She scribbled their names on the list, adding in '11' and '12' in the blank space at the bottom.

'Somehow I think the project might just survive without you, Chrissy,' Sarah said sarcastically. 'I don't think it *needs* you.'

Abi could see how annoyed Sarah was by Chrissy's performance. The two girls stood staring at each other for a few moments. Personally, Abi wouldn't want to cross either of them. At home, they called this 'a situation', and she had always made sure to steer well clear of situations.

Sarah and Chrissy continued to eyeball each other. It looked like Chrissy was trying to think of a witty comeback, but then gave up trying. She scowled at Sarah.

'Come on,' she said to her friends. 'I'm wasting time talking to the Nerd Herd.' Chrissy's little gang sniggered obediently. 'I know Miss Flood will want all of *us* in on this, there's simply no competition.' She flounced off down the corridor, closely followed by her friends.

When the door slammed shut behind them, Sarah, Hannah and Grace started laughing. Abi smiled nervously. Chrissy had put quite a dampener on what had been starting to look like Abi's best day so far at her new school.

'Way to go, Sarah,' Grace said, clapping her on the back.

Sarah grinned. 'She just drives me crazy,' she said, 'all that fake smiling and dressage this and dressage the other.' She shook her head. 'Chrissy's just such a . . . *girl*,' she said, as if that was the worst thing imaginable.

'Don't worry about Chrissy,' Hannah said to Abi, noticing that she'd gone quiet and looked a bit unsure about the whole exchange. Abi smiled gratefully at her and immediately felt like she could handle whatever school had to throw at her, once she had people like Hannah, Grace and Sarah to keep her sane.

'That Chrissy looks like she's taken with herself, that's for sure,' Abi said with a nod in the direction the girls had gone. 'And those clones have been totally suckered in.'

'Chrissy and the Clones!' Grace squealed. 'I love it.'

Abi blushed and started to say, 'I didn't mean to . . .' but Grace flung her arm round her and said, 'Don't apologize, I'm going to call them that from now on! Chrissy and the Clones – it's perfect.'

Hannah and Sarah were laughing now too. Abi let go of her worries and joined in.

'We were just heading home. Where do you live, Abi?' Hannah asked.

'In Elm View,' Abi said.

'That's near Sarah's house,' Hannah said, 'and not far from mine and Grace's. Do you fancy walking home together?'

'Sure,' Abi said quickly, happy to be included.

They left the school together and headed in the direction of Elm View. Hannah had an oddly shaped bag slung over her shoulder. Abi nodded at it. 'Do you play tennis,' she asked, 'or is that a musical instrument?'

'It's a racket,' Hannah said. 'Sarah's the musical one. I'm just a tennis player.'

'*Just*, yeah,' said Grace sarcastically. 'She's the school champ, Abi. She might even make the national team when she's older.'

'Oh, wow,' Abi said, surprised that someone who seemed quiet and into history and books would also be a good tennis player. 'That's so cool. I've got two left feet, so I'm no good at any sports.'

'And what about music?' Sarah asked. 'Do you play anything?'

'I'm trying to learn guitar,' Abi said with a shrug, 'but I think I might have two left hands as well.'

Sarah grinned at her. 'Stick at it, then you can accompany me when I'm playing the piano.'

'Maybe we can form a band,' Abi joked. 'Can either of you two sing?'

'Not well,' Grace said, 'but I'd be a brilliant front woman. I'd look the part!' They all laughed as Grace wiggled her hips like a model, her bangles jangling on her arm.

'So what was school like in Springfield?' Hannah asked, as they walked past the row of shops at the entrance to their estate.

'Um, different,' Abi said, not knowing where to begin. 'We call it middle school, for a start, and we have grades, not classes. It's more . . . I don't know . . . rigid, if you know what I mean and we get tons of homework.'

'Seriously?' said Sarah, arching her eyebrows. 'You cannot tell me any teacher in America gives more homework than Miss Flood.'

Abi laughed. 'She's a big softie compared to my old teachers!' Hannah shook her head in disbelief, and Sarah and Grace were open-mouthed at the thought.

'Did you mind moving here?' Grace asked.

Now Abi really didn't know where to begin. 'It was hard at first,' she said slowly, 'but I think I'm getting the hang of things. Girls like Chrissy make me feel a bit nervous because there were girls like that at home, but I think the museum thing sounds like fun. I'm glad I'll know you guys on the first day, though,' she added with a smile.

'It should be a good group, I think,' Grace said. 'Chrissy and her friends will obviously be a bit of a pain – you've met them now so you've probably guessed that yourself! Daniel and Jack are great, though, and very friendly. *Everyone* in our class is into Daniel,' she said, rolling her eyes. 'He's half-French and has big blue eyes, so you'll soon see why.'

Abi giggled. She hadn't noticed an incredibly cute guy around the place, but she'd definitely keep an eye out for him now!

'Josh can be a bit of a mean and moody type sometimes,' Grace went on, 'but he's OK really.'

'And Solomon plays tennis too,' Hannah added,

'and he seems really lovely. He's big into history, so I'm not surprised he signed up for it.'

'This is me,' Sarah said as they reached a set of white gates. 'See you all tomorrow.' She went down the driveway and into her house.

'Do you know where you are now?' Hannah asked Abi.

'Oh yeah, sure,' Abi said, nodding. 'I'm just the next block over.'

'Me and Grace are going back this way,' Hannah said, pointing in the opposite direction.

'OK,' Abi said with a smile. 'I guess I'll see you at school?'

'See you there!' Hannah beamed as Grace gave a big jangly wave goodbye and the two of them walked off, back up the road. Abi stood looking after them, smiling to herself. She was so glad she had put her name down on the list.

3

The Old Grainger House

'You know, girls, I'm really proud of you all for volunteering to do this.'

It was Saturday morning and Hannah's dad had offered to drop the four girls at the Grainger place on his way to the gym. Abi sat in the back seat with Grace and Sarah. Hannah was in the front, and Abi smiled to herself as she watched Hannah in the rear-view mirror, cringing as her father talked. She could relate – her own dad lectured her whenever he was driving her anywhere. Hannah looked like they couldn't get out of the car quick enough.

'It's very important to take these sorts of opportunities when they are presented to you,' Hannah's dad went on.

Abi felt Grace nudge her and looked across to see a wicked grin on Sarah's face as Hannah went redder and redder with embarrassment.

'I thought it was a shame when the old museum closed. It's great that your teacher is getting it going again. I always liked this place, in spite of what some people said about it.'

Abi looked up in interest. 'What did they say about it, Mr Greene?'

He shrugged. 'There was some nonsense about one of the Graingers being a witch and the place being haunted.'

'*What!*' Hannah said excitedly. 'Haunted?' She turned round in her seat to look at the girls. 'That would be amazing, wouldn't it!'

'Absolutely,' Grace said with a grin. 'I'd love a bit of ghost action. It would be hilarious!'

'Come on, Grace, really?' Sarah looked sceptical. 'That's just silly rumours.'

Hannah's dad was smiling to himself at their reactions, but Abi didn't know who to side with – her heart wanted to get excited with Hannah and Grace, while her head told her that Sarah was being sensible. But then imagine being in a real haunted house – and exploring it with these guys!

The car turned in at the main gates, which were tall and black and topped with spikes that looked like they meant business. Just beyond the gate, the road curved past a red-brick building with a sign on it that read: GRAINGER & SON & GRANDDAUGHTER, UNDERTAKERS AND FUNERAL PARLOUR.

'I'd say that's where most of the gossip came from,' Hannah's dad said, nodding towards the building. 'People can be a bit superstitious about undertakers.'

'Funny sign,' Abi said from the back seat. 'I've never seen "and Granddaughter" before.'

'I know, we must be the only town in the world with a sixteen-year-old undertaker,' Hannah's dad replied.

'*No way!*' Abi shrieked in disbelief.

'Seriously?' Sarah demanded. 'Are you saying there's an actual girl in there who's only four years older than us and spends all day with dead bodies?'

Hannah's dad laughed at their shocked faces. 'It's her family trade,' he said.

The girls looked at each other. Hanging out with the dead did not sound like a fun time.

'Um, you can just drop us here, Dad,' Hannah said suddenly, worried that her dad would embarrass her even more in front of the other volunteers.

'Thanks for the ride, Mr Greene,' said Abi, opening the door and hopping out of the car, with Grace and Sarah tumbling out behind her. Hannah practically leaped out of the front seat.

Hannah's dad rolled down his window. 'One more thing, girls.' They stopped and looked over at him. 'Don't get a fright when you meet the tree creatures.' He winked at them and drove off.

The girls looked at each other nervously. Abi wondered if he was teasing again and looked to Hannah for an explanation.

'Ignore him,' Hannah said firmly. 'He's just trying to be funny and failing. Miserably. Come on, let's get up to the house. It's nearly ten.'

'Did you hear about Chrissy?' Grace said as they walked quickly up the long, curving driveway. 'She couldn't get Tiffany and Sophie on the list after all. Miss Flood was having absolutely none of it. So it's just her and Elaine now.'

'Which one is Elaine again?' Abi asked.

'The one with the very curly brown hair and the wild look in her eye,' Grace said. 'She's like a trouble magnet. I think that's why she hangs out with Chrissy, because it means she'll always be at the centre of the drama.'

'I wonder how Elaine beat Tiffany and Sophie to become the chosen one,' Sarah said with a smirk. 'I bet she had to –' Sarah stopped abruptly and stared ahead.

'I bet she had to what?' Grace said, looking over at her. 'Sarah? What is it?'

Sarah raised her arm and pointed at the branches of a nearby tree. The other three girls looked to where she was pointing, and suddenly saw it. Abi gasped. A long, snake-like creature with a gargoyle head was curled round the branch, its face snarling down on any passers-by.

'Crikey,' breathed Grace, 'what's that?' She looked like she didn't want to move in case the creature decided to pounce.

There were all kinds of weird animals roaming about at home in America, so Abi decided to be brave and check it out for her friends. Moving very slowly, she inched her way towards the strange creature. It had a dead look in its eyes. She craned her neck to get a clearer look at it, then burst into relieved laughter.

'It's all right, guys,' she called over her shoulder, 'it's made of stone!'

'Are you absolutely sure?' Hannah whispered.

Abi marched up to the tree and reached up her hand to pat the snake-like body. 'Certain.' She grinned back at them.

'Phew,' said Grace. 'I was scared there, the undertakers' house was actually starting to look inviting.'

They broke into a fit of giggles and gathered round the tree, each reaching up to touch the cold, hard body of the unusual statue. From the gate, they heard the sound of bicycle wheels crunching over gravel.

Abi saw two boys come round the corner on their bikes, chatting to each other and oblivious to the girls up ahead.

'It's Jack and Daniel,' Sarah whispered. 'Hide! We'll be able to hear what they're saying!'

'Oh,' Grace said with a mischievous smile, 'and is there something in particular you'd like to hear from the lips of St Bruno's hottest boy, Sarah?'

Sarah blushed and stuck out her tongue at Grace. 'Of course not!' she hissed. 'Just hide. Quickly!'

The girls ducked behind tree trunks and crouched down, desperately trying to stifle their giggles.

Hannah leant close and whispered in Abi's ear. 'The boy on the left with brown spiky hair is Daniel – the one Sarah has a crush on.'

'*I do not!*'

'Shush!' Hannah giggled at Sarah's angry interruption. 'And the boy on the other bike with the red hair and freckles is Jack.'

The two boys were cycling along slowly and were close enough now that Abi could hear what they were saying.

'You know what's strange, though?' Jack said. 'Josh Fitzsimons has signed up for this. He hasn't exactly been friendly this year, has he? I wouldn't have thought he'd be into this. I mean, I didn't want to do it. I'm only here because you put my name down.'

Daniel grinned. 'You'll thank me for it. It should be fun hanging out with everyone outside of school for once.'

'Hanging out with *everyone* or hanging out with the *girls* who signed up to this?' Jack asked with a grin.

Out of the corner of her eye, Abi saw Sarah straining to hear what Daniel's answer would be. She smiled and crossed her fingers, hoping he'd say something about Sarah – he'd be crazy not to be into her, with her beautiful green eyes and long red hair. Abi thought Sarah was really gorgeous.

Before Daniel could answer, Jack suddenly jammed on his brakes and skidded to a halt.

'What the . . .?' he said, staring into the tree at the stone gargoyle.

Before he could figure out what it was, there was a sudden burst of music as Abi's mobile started to ring. Her ringtone was 'The Star-spangled Banner'. The girls looked at each other in horror as Abi grabbed the phone out of her pocket and punched the 'cancel call' button. Abi put her head in her hands and groaned.

'That seemed like such a cute idea when I downloaded it,' she whispered, her face red with embarrassment. 'I'm so sorry,' she said, shrugging helplessly.

'Hey, who's there?' Daniel demanded, looking in the direction of their hiding place.

The girls looked at each other, but there was nothing for it. They were rumbled. Slowly, they stood up and shuffled out awkwardly. Grace picked a few leaves out of her hair. Sarah looked like she wanted the ground to swallow her up.

Daniel and Jack looked at them in amusement. Without thinking, Abi opened her mouth and babbled, 'We, uh, we were looking for, like, more of those ugly gargoyle things . . .'

'Right . . .' said Jack with a grin.

'No, really,' Hannah said, nodding. 'We thought there might be more of them because my dad said something about tree *creatures*, so this can't be the only one.'

Jack and Daniel exchanged a look, but said nothing. Daniel stepped closer and looked at the stone animal's wide eyes and gaping mouth. 'This one is really ugly, isn't it?' he said.

'Yeah, I know,' Abi said, relieved that he'd decided not to ask any questions about what they were doing, crouched down in the dirt. She felt so silly, hiding like a first grader. The other girls looked very embarrassed too. In an attempt to save face, she changed the subject. 'Hannah, your dad also said there were rumours about the house being haunted, but that's just nonsense, right? You don't really go in for all that over here, do you?'

'You think ghosts and scary things only go to America?' Sarah said with a grin.

'Well, we seem to get all the aliens,' Abi said, 'so why not the ghosts too?'

They all burst out laughing at that, even Daniel and Jack. Abi blushed, but she was delighted. Back home, nobody ever laughed at her jokes.

'This is Abi,' Grace said. 'She's new to town and she's in Miss Carson's class.'

'I am too,' Jack said, smiling at her. 'I've been meaning to go over and say hello to you.'

'Nice to meet you,' Daniel said politely. Abi was amazed by his manners – her friends at home would laugh themselves stupid if they heard a boy talking like that.

'Well, I don't know about you lot, but I reckon the place does look a bit spooky,' Jack said, pointing through a gap in the trees ahead.

The girls hadn't even noticed the first glimpse of the house at the top of the wide, sloping driveway. Through the trees, in the distance, they could see a long, grey house with lots of windows and chimney pots. At either end a wall curved out, hiding the back of the building from view. The house looked like it was waiting for something, like it was staring out over the landscape expectantly.

It's waiting for us, Abi suddenly thought to herself. Then she shook her head and laughed at herself for being so dramatic. It was just a big old house.

4

Looking Around

Outside the Grainger house, Miss Flood was standing with the other volunteers. Abi could see Chrissy and Elaine standing to one side, whispering and giggling together. One boy was studying the house, obviously very interested in the building. Another boy was slouched against the wall beside the door and looked like he didn't want to talk to anyone. Once the girls and Jack and Daniel had joined them, Miss Flood unlocked the heavy front door and pushed it open. Abi felt a shiver of anticipation.

They stepped through into the wide reception hall and were greeted by a slightly musty smell and a heavy air of deep silence. It felt wrong to make any noise at all, like they were intruders in a place where they didn't belong.

Miss Flood went off to find the main power switch and told them to have a look around. The volunteers stood together uncertainly, not moving, staring at the wooden doors that stood at intervals round the hall.

'Shall we . . . go into one of the rooms?' asked the boy who had been introduced to Abi as Solomon. He was the one who had been studying the house. Now, he sounded a little nervous.

They glanced at each other, but still no one moved.

'I'll do it,' said someone with an impatient sigh. It was the slouching boy Abi had noticed outside. He had floppy dark hair and even darker eyes. She caught his eye for a second before he looked away and headed for the nearest door.

'Who's that, Hannah?' Abi asked her friend.

'Josh Fitzsimons,' Hannah replied, looking at Abi with curiosity. 'He's a bit intense, but he's nice when you get to know him. I've know him since we were five,' she said.

Abi watched Josh grab the handle and swing the door open. 'Sitting room,' he called over his shoulder. The rest of the volunteers all trooped in behind him.

'Oh, it's gorgeous,' said Grace. 'I expected dust covers and mothballs.'

The room was large and bright, with a big stone fireplace, a line of long windows showing a view of the garden beyond and a scattering of mismatched sofas and chairs. Heavy green drapes were caught back on either side of the windows. The volunteers wandered around, touching the lamps, testing the chairs and craning their necks at the windows to see as much of the garden as they could.

'It feels a bit strange, doesn't it?' said Jack suddenly.

'Strange how?' said Sarah, frowning at him.

'Well,' said Jack, looking around the room, 'I keep expecting to find someone sitting here having tea or something, ready to shout at us to get out of their house.'

'A very good description, Jack,' Miss Flood said, as she walked into the room to join them. 'You all know how much I love living history, and this place is living history to me. I know exactly what you mean, Jack – it's like stepping back in time.'

They walked from room to room, looking at everything. Abi hung back from the group and took it all in. She'd never been in a place like this before, but she loved it immediately. On the ground floor there was the wide reception area, a billiards room, a gunroom near the back door, a small library, a sitting room, a ballroom and a drawing room that was full of furniture and interesting-looking objects dumped there from elsewhere in the house. The ceilings in the rooms were high and the windows were long, and everywhere there was old furniture and beautiful ornaments. There seemed to be a wide stone fireplace in every room.

An ornate staircase led up from the ground floor

to the first and second floors. On the first floor they went in and out of bedrooms, washrooms, dressing rooms, a nursery and a schoolroom. Everything was still in place – beds, washstands, wardrobes, desks and chairs. Jack was right, it really did feel like the family had just gone outside and would be back in a minute. It was an odd feeling to be walking around in the silence, opening and closing doors that led to past lives and forgotten memories.

'Now I'll show you the kitchens,' Miss Flood called out. 'They're in the basement.'

They walked down the ornate staircase, then round to a small corridor from which led a set of plain wooden stairs. This brought them down into the main kitchen, and when they saw it there was a collective gasp of amazement. The kitchen walls were crammed with shelves filled with pots and pans and odd gadgets, a massive butcher's-block table stood in the centre of the floor and to one side was a sink that was big enough to be a child's bath. The fireplace was cavernous, with pots and pans hanging above it and a meat rack that folded out of the wall on one side. It was so wide that six of them could stand inside it in a row.

Miss Flood beamed at their reaction. 'So,' she said, 'what do you think? Are you looking forward to bringing this place back to life as a working museum?'

Abi looked around and wondered what it would

take to get the house up and running as a place for people to visit. It seemed like a lot of work, whichever way you looked at it. She was about to ask, but Sarah got in before her.

'When you say a "working museum", do you mean ready so that people will actually *pay* to come here?'

'Yes, of course,' replied Miss Flood.

Silence.

'So not only will we have to clean it up, prepare exhibits in all the rooms and finally open it up but also actually give tours?'

'Exactly,' Miss Flood said, smiling at her.

Deathly silence.

'Er, Miss,' Sarah said, frowning, 'you do realize we're only twelve?'

Miss Flood laughed. 'Yes, of course I do, but we're well able to do this. Now, who has any ideas to get us started and to get this place re-opened as a brand-new museum?'

Hannah and Daniel both started to speak at the same time. 'Sorry, Hannah, you go first,' Daniel said.

'Thanks, Daniel. I, um, was just going to say, it might be a good idea to write up explanation cards to go with the exhibits,' Hannah said. 'That way visitors will know what they're looking at.'

'Excellent idea,' agreed Miss Flood. 'And you, Daniel?'

'What about a soundtrack for some of the rooms? I was thinking we could play recordings of, like, children saying their lessons in the schoolroom or the noises of a busy kitchen down here.'

'You could do that?' Miss Flood said in surprise.

Daniel shrugged. 'Sure, I think so. With an iPod and some speakers it shouldn't be hard to rig up.'

'I could probably help with that,' Josh said stiffly, without looking at anyone.

Josh seemed so different from the other boys that were volunteering. It was obvious some of the others thought he was a bit rude, but Abi wasn't sure about that.

'That's a fantastic idea,' Miss Flood said, interrupting Abi's thoughts. 'Will both of you boys look into that and let me know what you'd need. In fact, if we –' She stopped suddenly, mid-sentence. 'Did anyone else hear a noise?' she asked.

The group went quiet as everyone listened intently. Abi shivered.

'I heard that,' Solomon whispered. 'What was it?' The noise grew louder, a shuffling sound that moved about above their heads.

'Oh, come on, you losers. It's obviously just a mouse or something,' Chrissy scoffed, examining her nails.

'I can definitely hear something quite heavy moving about upstairs.' Elaine sounded a lot less sure.

'But I locked the front door.' Miss Flood was whispering now too.

'It's heading for the stairs,' Grace whispered.

Sure enough, the soft *shuffle-shuffle* was making its way to the top of the stairs that led down to the kitchen. Everyone stared at the steps, waiting. Slowly, the noise moved on to the top step, then came a soft *thud* as it moved down, one step at a time. They braced themselves for whatever apparition was going to appear before them. *Shuffle – thud. Shuffle – thud. Shuffle – thud.*

'Hello?' boomed a voice.

Abi clapped her hand to her mouth to stifle a scream.

'Anyone here?'

'Oh! It's just Mr Grainger, everybody,' Miss Flood announced shakily to the volunteers. Abi looked at Hannah's pale face and at Solomon gripping the table edge, and she knew she wasn't alone in being very relieved. 'We're here,' Miss Flood called out.

A pair of slippers came into view, quickly followed by a belt, a waistcoat, then a kind face with spectacles and a warm smile.

'I wasn't expecting you until later, Mr Grainger,' Miss Flood said, standing up to greet him.

He looked around at the ten pale faces gazing up at him and gave a little laugh. 'I did wonder why you all looked like you'd seen a ghost. Has the old place been playing tricks on you?'

They looked at one another sheepishly and Grace mumbled something about that being a silly idea.

Mr Grainger grinned at them, then looked back up the stairs and called out, 'Come on down here, my dear.'

A striking figure descended into view. She was wearing a purple-and-black dress over black tights and a pair of laced-up boots. Her glossy black hair hung down in a heavy fringe over her eyes. There was a tiny silver stud in her nose. Beside her, Abi could hear Grace sigh in delight at this vision in black – someone who liked dressing up as much as she did, obviously. All Abi could think of was Dracula – or rather, Dracula's wife. The girl in black stared around the kitchen, looking from one to the other, like she was daring them to say something to her. No one said a word.

'This is my daughter, Simone,' Mr Grainger said.

Grace nudged Abi and whispered, 'She must be the undertaker!'

'Her dad's quite old, isn't he?' Abi whispered back. Her own dad went running every day and was always talking about looking ten years younger than his age – which was a big deal to him. But Mr Grainger had definitely never been introduced to a bottle of hair-dye, or men's moisturiser for that matter!

'Hello, Simone, it's lovely to mee–' Miss Flood began.

But Jack couldn't contain himself any longer. 'So, Simone, do you actually . . . work with . . . dead people?' he said, failing to keep the grisly interest out of his voice. Abi realized that she, Hannah, Grace and Sarah weren't the only ones to have been told about the family business before this trip. They probably weren't the only ones to have heard rumours about ghosts either, judging by how nervously everyone had reacted to Mr Grainger's footsteps.

'Jack!' scolded Miss Flood, shooting him a warning look.

Simone's bright blue, kohl-rimmed eyes came to rest on him. 'No, it's OK, Miss Flood,' she said quietly. 'What do you want to know . . . exactly, Jack?'

'Oh, no . . . I . . . um . . . Just . . . you know,' Jack stammered. 'It just seems . . .'

'Crazy?' she said in that same quiet voice.

Jack blushed to the roots of his hair. 'No, of course not,' he said quickly. 'I don't think it sounds crazy. It sounds deadly.' Abi cringed for him as she saw him realize too late what he'd said. 'No, not deadly,' he said quickly. 'Sorry, I mean . . . brilliant.'

Simone shook her head and smiled, in spite of herself.

'Oh yeah, right,' Chrissy said loudly. 'Like you *actually* think it's brilliant, Jack Bateman. It *does* sound crazy. Completely crazy. No girl wants to be with dead people all day long, I mean, come on! That is *not* normal. Am I right?'

'You're right, all right,' Elaine said quickly, relishing the chance to cause a stir and suck up to Chrissy.

The mask slipped back down over Simone's face and her expression darkened. She folded her arms and set her mouth in a tight line.

Before Abi's brain knew what was happening, her mouth had opened and started speaking angrily. 'That is totally rude. Apologize to her!' Abi burst out. The others stared at her in surprise. She couldn't believe she'd actually said that out loud herself. She bit her lip and looked at her new friends, hoping they wouldn't hate her for being so outspoken. She needn't have worried – Grace, Hannah and Sarah were looking at her proudly, and she knew they'd support her all the way. The others just looked shocked – all except Josh. He was watching her with a half-smile on his face. Abi couldn't tell what he was thinking.

Chrissy, meanwhile, had walked over and planted herself squarely in front of Abi. 'Apologize to this . . . *weirdo*? Does she look normal to you?' she demanded, not waiting for Abi to answer. 'No, she doesn't; she looks like someone let out of the asylum on day release.'

Elaine sniggered. Abi's jaw fell open – she was so taken aback by Chrissy's rudeness. It was off the scale! Grace managed to find the words first. 'Chrissy, that is a dreadful thing to say,' she said, clearly biting back her anger. 'If you want to attack someone for how they dress, stick with me. Leave Simone out of it.'

Chrissy flicked back her dark hair. 'Oh, please,' she said, in full drama-queen mode now. '*Hello?* I'm just stating the obvious here, although I can see why someone like *you* would defend someone like *her*. And for your information –'

'Enough,' snapped Miss Flood. They all froze. They knew the dangerous tone of that voice all too well. 'Chrissy Edwards, upstairs. *Now,*' Miss Flood said firmly, then turned on her heel and walked briskly up the stairs. Chrissy stalked after her. The others looked at each other, unsure what to say next.

'Well,' said Mr Grainger quietly, 'I think that charming young girl has a bright future in the caring professions.' Everyone burst out laughing. Elaine folded her arms across her chest and refused to join in. Abi giggled uncontrollably, glad to have the tension broken, but still shaking from her unexpected burst of anger.

Grace walked over to the Graingers and stuck out her hand, bracelets jangling. 'Hello, I'm Grace, and it's lovely to meet you.' Simone and her father shook hands, working their way round the rest of the room as each person introduced themselves.

Elaine shot Simone a dark look as she quickly shook her hand and then dropped it, as if she had some horrible disease. When Simone reached Abi, she looked her straight in the eye. Abi smiled at her.

'Sorry about all that,' Abi said. 'That girl was so rude, but I shouldn't have turned it into such a big thing.'

Simone smiled back, her blue eyes twinkling with humour, making her look very like her dad, Mr Grainger. 'That's all right,' she said. 'I thoroughly enjoyed it, actually. I don't think anyone's ever stood up for me like that before.'

The two girls grinned at each other.

Miss Flood and Chrissy came back five minutes later and Chrissy mumbled a very insincere apology to Simone, who said nothing. Abi didn't think Chrissy really deserved a response.

'Why don't we go up to the sitting room, and then Mr Grainger is going to tell you a little bit about the house,' Miss Flood suggested.

They all headed back up the stairs and made themselves comfortable on the sofas in the sitting room. Mr Grainger sat in an armchair, and for the next hour he regaled them with tales from his unusual childhood in the house, even describing secret corridors and hidey-holes. He talked about the servants and the visitors who arrived without warning – like the young Russian count who decided to nurse a broken heart there and ended up staying three years. Abi thought it sounded fascinating.

'My parents, Beryl and Audoen Grainger, donated the house to the town about forty years ago. The family's fortunes changed and they couldn't afford to keep it up any more. About twelve years ago, the town council opened it as a local heritage museum, but funding ran out after only eighteen months and they closed it down again. So for the last ten years I've been acting as a caretaker for the old place and become quite resigned to it remaining unused. That is until Miss Flood here came along,' he said, smiling at her. 'She has managed to find a patron, Eliza Wells, who is prepared to donate an annual sum to run the house as a museum. Miss Wells has a long association with the house, dating back to when her sister worked here as a housekeeper. Her money is very welcome, but it's not very much, which is why you volunteers are so important. We couldn't do this without you, so I'd like to thank you for giving your time. Now, have you seen everything?'

'We've seen all the rooms on all three floors,' Hannah said. 'It's huge.'

'What about outside?' Mr Grainger asked. 'The Rose Garden, the Ladies' Walk, the Mausoleum?'

They shook their heads.

'Well then, how about you give them the guided tour, Simone?'

'Fantastic!' said Grace, grinning delightedly at Simone, who looked like she'd rather walk over a bed of nails barefoot than walk them around the place. Abi reckoned she probably dreaded spending more time than she had to with Chrissy and Elaine.

Chrissy put up her hand. 'Yes?' Mr Grainger asked.

'What's a mausoleum?' Chrissy asked with a frown. 'It sounds weird.'

'It's a burial house for the Graingers,' Simone replied. 'I eat my lunch in there most days, actually, with my family, so to speak.' She looked directly at Chrissy with a wicked glint in her eye as she said this. Chrissy stared at her, clearly trying to weigh up whether she was telling the truth or not, but either way she knew better than to chance another outburst in Miss Flood's presence.

Abi had to bite her lip to stop herself from laughing out loud. Josh, on the other hand, obviously wasn't bothered what Chrissy thought of him because he laughed loudly. Abi looked at him in surprise and saw Simone glance at him and smile quickly. Abi looked over at Chrissy, who looked red-faced and furious. Abi saw her lean over and whisper something into Elaine's ear, then the two of them marched off towards the back door.

Sarah winked at Abi, Hannah and Grace and said quietly, 'Well, this should be a seriously interesting tour.'

5

The Mausoleum

The volunteers left the kitchen and grabbed their jackets on the way to the back door. Simone led them up a few steps and out through a door leading into the back courtyard. A stone path, slippy with moss, brought them down to an arch in the curved hedge wall that separated the garden from the courtyard. Only the family and their guests would have been allowed through here – apart from the team of gardeners needed to maintain it. The path branched to the left, on to a Ladies' Walk of rhododendrons and lavender plants. The garden was a huge circle, so the stone path looped around its outer perimeter, with access points cut into the hedge along the way. The first two-thirds of the circle, nearest the house, were taken up by an extensive kitchen garden. Following Simone, they walked the curving path, past sculptures and a large Gothic tower that Simone called a folly, past the Lovers' Arbour and the Rose Garden.

Abi was falling more and more in love with this

place with each step she took. It was amazing. She looked over at Hannah, who was walking beside her and looked to be almost in a daze of delight.

'I'd love to live here,' Abi whispered to Hannah.

'Oh my God, I know,' Hannah said breathlessly. 'I feel like I'm going to stumble upon Emily Brontë sitting on a bench, dreaming up Heathcliff.'

'Heathcliff?' Abi asked, puzzled at the unfamiliar name.

Hannah shook her head. 'And I thought Sarah and Grace were bad!' she teased. 'You cannot have not heard of *Wuthering Heights*, please tell me it's not true.'

Abi blushed. 'Uh, well, I . . .'

'I'm going to lend you a copy. I think you'll love it,' Hannah said with a grin. 'Don't even bother trying to argue with me.'

Before Abi could say any more, Simone cut across them.

'There's the labyrinth,' she said, gesturing to the left. They turned to look at the archway cut in the hedge and could see that it led into a hedge tunnel that turned sharply right and disappeared from view.

'An actual labyrinth?' asked Sarah. 'Can we have a go?' She started towards the entrance, but Simone called her back.

'No can do, Sarah,' she said, shaking her head. 'If you get lost in there, your teacher and my father will not be impressed.'

Daniel grinned at Sarah's enthusiasm. 'We can bring you a ball of wool to unravel as you go. Maybe you'll be the first person to ever find the centre.'

Sarah smiled at Daniel, but before she could answer, Chrissy elbowed between them. 'Or maybe,' she said with a sneer, 'she'll be lost in there forever and one day they'll find a skeleton holding a ball of wool.'

Sarah glowered at her.

'Come on. This way,' Simone said, gesturing for everyone to follow her.

'Wow!' they heard Grace shout excitedly from up ahead. 'Look at this place.'

When they reached her, the volunteers stared in disbelief. In front of them was a graveyard, with miniature but perfectly carved Gothic gravestones. Most were only about three feet high, but they had turrets and stone wreaths and even mini gargoyles. It was like a horror movie for kids.

'Don't tell me they buried the poor servants here?' gasped Grace.

Simone laughed behind her hand. 'No, this is the pet cemetery.'

'This was for animals?' Jack said, looking around in wonder. 'Were they nuts? It must have cost a fortune to make all these headstones.'

'It did,' Simone said, looking at the ornate carvings, 'but they felt their pets deserved it.'

'No wonder people thought the family was a bit strange,' Elaine stage-whispered loudly to Chrissy. 'Til death do us part is not something you usually say to your dog!' Chrissy sniggered. Abi saw Simone turn her back on them.

They followed the path onwards again until they reached an avenue of yew trees. They walked under the trees and emerged in a clearing, facing a squat, red-brick building with the name 'Grainger' carved over the wooden door in large letters. It had a simple pitched roof, but no windows, and ivy was making its way slowly up from the ground towards the roof tiles. On the side wall was a large carving of a skull, with worms crawling out of the eye sockets.

'That's horrible,' said Chrissy with a shudder.

Simone smiled. 'It's a *memento mori*,' she said.

'Translate, Hannah,' Sarah said.

'Reminder of death,' Hannah said, staring intently at the carving.

'You know Latin?' Abi looked at Hannah, her eyes wide with admiration.

Hannah shrugged. 'No, I just read a lot so I pick things up here and there.'

Abi was about to say something else, when Sarah put her hand on her arm. 'I know,' she said, 'it's a little unnerving, but you'll get used to Hannah and her book-eating brain.'

Hannah smiled at Sarah in delight. 'Oliver Jeffers. Well done, Sarah!'

Sarah raised her eyebrows and looked at Abi. 'No, I've no idea either,' she said, making Abi dissolve into a fit of giggles.

'Hannah's right,' Simone interrupted them. 'A *memento mori* is meant to remind the living that they too will die, so they should live good lives. It's a warning that life is short and death spares no one.'

'Cool,' Jack whispered, mostly to himself. Chrissy and Elaine made a face behind his back.

They all stared at the carving in silence and Abi could feel the hairs stand up on the back of her neck. She wasn't normally affected by graveyards, but this little dead house hidden in the trees and the skull with the worms gave her the creeps. She took a few steps back, so she wasn't looking at the skull any more.

Suddenly, Solomon let out a shout of terror. Everyone jumped; Elaine screamed.

'What's wrong?' Simone said quickly.

Solomon pointed at the tree beside the mausoleum. 'I'm sorry,' he said, 'it's just one of those . . . things . . . creatures. Suddenly it was there – I didn't see it before.'

Simone stared at him for a moment. 'It's a statue,' she said pointedly.

Solomon was still staring at the creature. This one had a body like a fox, a snake's tail and a face twisted into a terrifying grimace. It was staring right at them. 'But – it wasn't there before,' he said, sounding confused. 'Then I looked back and –'

'It's a statue,' Simone repeated. 'As in an inanimate object. So can we ignore it now, please, and get this little tour over and done with?'

Solomon nodded silently, but his eyes never left the statue. Hannah patted his arm. 'They are freaky, Sol,' she said gently, 'but I'm sure it was there all along and you just didn't notice it.' Solomon didn't look so sure.

The wind was gusting stronger now, whipping the girls' hair across their faces and making the boys dig their hands deeper into their pockets. Dark clouds overhead were threatening rain. Simone pulled a heavy brass key out of her pocket. 'Ready to greet the dead?' she said mischievously.

'Well, at least you're dressed for it,' Chrissy muttered.

Abi sighed. She felt bad for Simone and was getting sick of Chrissy's snide remarks.

'Maybe there'll be thunder and lightning and we'll have to stay in here for a while,' Jack said, rubbing his hands together. 'This is a bit like that film where the kids get lost in the woods when they're camping, isn't it? And then they all get eaten by a werewolf.'

Simone gave a little laugh. 'That's the spirit,' she said to Jack. 'And if we need to send out people to face the werewolf I think Elaine and Chrissy would do a wonderful job.'

Abi and the girls giggled to each other as Elaine and Chrissy looked like they would happily feed Simone to a pack of wolves.

Simone pushed the heavy key into the lock and turned it twice. Abi was surprised to see Josh step forward to help her, putting his weight against the door. With rusty reluctance, the hinges creaked into motion and the door inched open. They all peered into the gloom of the mausoleum. Simone switched on the torch she'd borrowed from Miss Flood and stepped inside. The volunteers crowded in behind her.

The mausoleum was large enough for all of them to stand together in the centre of it. Simone slowly turned the torch's beam across the room. On their right, a series of five shelves ran up the wall, with an urn standing in the middle of each one. On their left, a number of coffins were stacked, one on top of the other, each separated from the next by a thin slab of concrete. The air was dusty and dry. They looked up as they heard *plink, plink, plink* above their heads – the rain had started and was spattering against the roof.

'This is incredible,' whispered Abi, looking around. 'I've never been in a mausoleum before. Can you tell us about it, Simone?'

'The burials date back to 1774,' Simone began

to explain, her voice echoing oddly against the cold stone walls, 'and the first was Millicent Grainger, who was buried in the bottom coffin, there. That was followed by six more coffin burials. The ashes of five Graingers are stored in the urns on the shelf. So there are twelve of my ancestors entombed here.'

'Don't you mean thirteen?' Grace said in a puzzled voice.

'No, twelve,' Simone replied.

Grace looked from the urns to the coffins. 'But . . . there are *eight* coffins and five urns,' she said slowly. 'Look.'

Simone sighed impatiently, but used the light to count the urns – five – then the coffins. She looked confused, then bent down to count the coffins again. 'Hey, you're right, Grace,' she said, surprised. 'Those two there aren't separated by a concrete slab, so it looks like just one coffin. Actually, the bottom one is getting damaged from the weight of the other.' She straightened up. 'I can't believe it,' she said, shaking her head. 'I've always been told there are twelve burials. It even says so in the book about my family in the library up at the house.' She shook her head again, frowning. 'I'll have to check it with my dad,' she said, staring at the coffins.

As their eyes grew accustomed to the gloomy light, they didn't need the triangle of light provided by the torch to make out the stone carvings on the end wall – the family crest and an egg-timer – and the fact that there were some words engraved on the floor.

'What does that say?' Abi asked, fascinated, pointing at the floor.

Simone turned round. '*Non omnis moriar*,' she said, 'which means, "I shall not wholly die", or "Not all of me will die". It's a quote from a poem by Horace, who was a poet in Ancient Rome.'

'And why the egg-timer?' asked Jack, pointing to the wall carving.

'That's another *memento mori*, like the skull outside,' Simone explained. 'It's telling us that time is ticking, that our time on earth is short.'

'They really wanted to hammer home that point, didn't they?' Jack muttered.

The others laughed but Abi had just seen something that stopped her in her tracks. 'Oh my goodness,' she breathed, feeling very afraid.

Hannah looked up quickly and moved over beside her. 'Abi, what is it? Are you OK?' she whispered.

Sarah and Grace joined them, their faces creased with worry as they looked at Abi, pale and staring. She looked completely rattled.

'Eh, you're all picture and no sound there, Abi,' Sarah said quietly. 'What's wrong?'

'Look' was all Abi could manage to say as she nodded towards the end wall. Her three friends turned and peered into the murky half-light at the end of the mausoleum.

'What the . . .?' Grace's eyes widened and Sarah stood stock still, her mouth wide open. Hannah was fixed to the spot, unable to tear her eyes away from the corner of the mausoleum.

Glancing back for a second, it was obvious to Abi that no one else could see what they were seeing. There in the corner, between the coffin wall and the end wall, stood a young girl, deathly pale, wearing a long, white lace dress with a gauze veil falling down her back. In her hands she held a withered posy of flowers and a piece of paper. Her eyes were mournful and pleading. Abi could feel her heart beating like crazy in her chest. Was this for real?

Simone flicked the torchlight towards the door, pointing out another small wall carving to the others, and the end of the room was swallowed up by darkness once more. The four girls looked at each other, suddenly doubting they had seen anything at all. They slowly shifted themselves, unclenching their muscles and breathing again. But just a moment later they became aware of a strange sound, like a soft rustling. It started as a whisper in the corner and built up slowly until it reached their ears. The noise was soft but unmistakable: someone was crying in the gloom.

'OK, I think that concludes your little tour,'

Simone said, breaking into their bewildered thoughts. 'Let's get back to the house.'

'The rain is getting heavier,' Daniel called from the doorway. 'Shall we stay or go, Simone?'

'GO!' Sarah said, far too loudly.

Simone turned and looked at the four girls suspiciously. She frowned, but didn't say anything about the four terrified faces in front of her. 'Come on then,' she said to the group and everyone made a break for it, running out into the rain.

Abi, Grace, Sarah and Hannah quickly overtook everyone else as they sprinted ahead, running as if their lives depended on it.

6

The Writing Room

The following Saturday morning, the volunteers arrived at the Grainger house in old clothes, ready to get dusty and dirty. All except Grace, of course, who was wearing her own version of workwear: a battered pair of denim dungarees that she had decorated with painted flowers and beads, with a flowery shirt underneath, her favourite pink Converse and her hair tied up, turban-style. Abi grinned when she saw her – she loved the way that Grace had her own style and wasn't afraid to dress as she liked.

The girls had decided to cycle this time, and they approached the house slowly on their bikes. Abi felt a bit reluctant at the idea of going back in there, but Hannah, Grace and Sarah hadn't said a word about what had happened in the mausoleum last week. It was as if they had made a silent agreement to just ignore it, and they had all honoured that agreement for the whole week in school. It was a bit harder now, though, faced with the house looming up in front of them.

'OK, stop,' Sarah called out suddenly. The four bikes braked to a halt. 'Are we going to mention . . . it?' Sarah asked.

'I was just thinking the same thing,' Abi admitted. 'I know we haven't said anything but, I mean . . . what happened last week?'

Hannah shrugged and looked down at her feet. 'I don't know,' she said quietly. 'I was planning on putting it out of my mind and never asking that question.'

'What do you think, Grace?' Sarah asked.

'Well, I'm into science,' Grace said slowly, 'and what we think we saw doesn't make sense.'

'So,' Hannah said hopefully, 'you're saying it was probably just a trick of the light?'

Grace nodded. 'Yeah, and a trick of the wind. You know, the crying bit.'

Abi couldn't meet her friends' eyes. She was so confused about the whole thing, but, at the same time, what they were saying was sensible.

'Right,' said Sarah firmly, 'so we're all agreed that it was a trick of the light and the wind and it was nothing really?'

Grace nodded in agreement. Hannah didn't look so convinced, but she nodded too. Abi looked from one girl to the other. She opened her mouth to say something, but then changed her mind. She nodded.

'Good,' said Sarah with relief. 'Then we'll just forget that it ever happened.'

They made their way over to the bicycle stands and locked their bikes, then headed inside the house. As they crossed the threshold, Abi felt a shiver run down her spine.

Stop being silly, she said to herself sternly. *It's just a house.*

In the reception area, Miss Flood was drawing up a list of rooms and jobs. The other volunteers were already there, standing in front of her in a semicircle.

'We're going to split up today and tackle some of the rooms,' Miss Flood announced. 'Does anyone want any particular room?'

Sarah raised her hand. 'I've an idea for the schoolroom,' she said. 'I'd like to check in the cupboards there and see if there are any props we could use to set it up. Do you want to help me, Grace?'

'Sure,' Grace replied.

Daniel and Josh went off to plan the soundtrack, with Chrissy and Elaine trailing after them. 'We'd love to help too, Daniel,' Chrissy said in her girliest voice. Grace mimed a flouncy Chrissy-style walk as she made her way towards the stairs. Abi had to bite her hand to stop herself from shouting with laughter.

'Looks like we're partners, then,' Jack said to Solomon.

'Looks like it,' Solomon said with a grin. 'Do you want to start in the kitchen?'

'Sure,' said Jack and they headed towards the back stairs.

'Come on, Abi,' said Hannah, 'how about we start in the drawing room? It's become a bit of a dumping ground – there must be stuff for all the rooms in there. If we find any schoolroom things,' she shouted after Grace and Sarah as they scooted up the stairs, 'we'll bring them up to you.'

They crossed over to the drawing room, which was a wide, high-ceilinged room with a very large glass chandelier.

'This is amazing,' Abi said as they stepped inside. 'It's like going into Aladdin's cave.' She looked around the room, which was crammed with bits of furniture and strange-looking objects that she couldn't recognize. 'What's this?' she asked, holding up something that looked a bit like a frying pan, but, instead of being open, it was enclosed by two metal halves joined together. She held it by the handle and turned it round, wondering what it could be.

Hannah looked up from the letter opener she was examining and shrugged. 'Beats me,' she said. 'Maybe it's a . . . tadpole catcher? You know, you scoop them up in that and leave them in it to become frogs and then . . . cook them on the fire and eat them?' she suggested.

'Eeeew!' Abi started laughing. 'You certainly wouldn't get anything like that back home!' she said, shaking her head. Then she spotted something peeking out from behind a beautiful wooden table. It looked like an old-fashioned loudhailer. She went over and tugged it out. 'Oh wow, Hannah, come here and look at this. It's an old . . . whaddya-call-it.'

Hannah raised an eyebrow. 'Abi, the sooner we de-Americanize you, the better. We have a perfectly good word for that. It's a gramophone.'

'That's it,' said Abi, 'I just couldn't think of it. It's beautiful, isn't it? How old do you think it is?'

'Must be about a hundred years, I suppose,' Hannah said. 'I think they had something like that in *Little Women*. Or maybe not – they just gathered round the piano, right?'

The gramophone had a wooden box as its base and from it rose a tall, curving horn speaker that widened out into the familiar loudhailer shape. It looked like a strange flower bursting out in springtime.

'You know something,' Abi said, 'I bet we could make a ton of money if we had a garage sale for all this stuff.' There was no reply from Hannah, except a strangled cough. 'No, really, Hannah, I mean it,' Abi said, still staring at the gramophone. 'I'd say there's people would pay a whole lot to get their hands on this stuff.'

Another strangled cough. Abi looked over at her friend, who was staring at her oddly. 'Do you need a lozenge or something, Hannah?'

Hannah sighed impatiently. 'No, Abi, I don't need a lozenge. That was my *there's a teacher right behind you shut up* face.'

Abi's hand flew to her mouth and she spun round to find Miss Flood standing just behind her. 'Oh Jeez, I didn't mean that, Miss Flood. I mean, I was just joking, I would never . . .'

Miss Flood folded her arms. 'So, Miss Worthy, should I expect to see the town's proud heritage as a job lot on eBay any time soon?'

Abi blushed fiercely. 'Oh no, Miss Flood. I promise I . . .'

Miss Flood put her hand on Abi's arm and laughed. 'You're all right, Abi. I know you're only joking. You have a very good eye, though. That is an expensive item. It's an Edison Home Phonograph, dating to around 1910. It's an early record-player, I suppose you'd call it. You had to be wealthy to have one of these in your house back then. Actually, I know someone who'll be very interested to see that.' She stuck her head out of the door and shouted Grace's name. There was the sound of running feet overhead, then down the staircase, and Grace hurtled through the door. 'Yes, Miss?'

'I thought you'd like to have a look at this, Grace, you being a science boffin.'

She stood back and Grace caught sight of the phonograph. 'Crikey,' she said, approaching it as if it was an injured baby bird. She reached out to

53

run her fingers very gently along the curving shell of the speaker horn. 'That's an Edison,' she breathed, eyes wide with delight.

Grace and Miss Flood started to discuss the machine in detail, heads bent together as they examined it. Hannah and Abi exchanged a glance. 'And I thought you were the nerd,' Abi said with a giggle.

'I am when it comes to books,' Hannah said, grinning, 'but no one is as into science as Grace. She's the great white hope of the science teacher. I think he pictures her winning a Nobel prize or something and dedicating it to him.' She moved off to the end of the room, her eye caught by a silver box on the floor near the window. She scrambled over the furniture, making her way towards it.

'I'm really surprised they had one,' Grace was saying. 'Does the family know who bought it?'

'Yes, and that's the exciting thing,' said Miss Flood. 'I asked Mr Grainger about it and he said it was bought by one of the family around 1911.'

Grace gasped. 'So it's a genuine original?'

Miss Flood nodded. 'Well, if he's right, it is. He told me that his great-great-grandmother, Celia Grainger, had a son called Henry and he used his wealth to educate himself about these sorts of new gadgets and acquire them. So it's been in the family since then.'

'Miss,' Abi called suddenly, 'there's another unusual gadget over here that might have been Henry's too.' Miss Flood turned round, full of interest, as Abi picked up the 'tadpole catcher'. She held it up. 'We've no idea what it is, but if he loved new technology, perhaps it's something important, and not for catching tadpoles like Hannah thought?'

Miss Flood stared at the object, then at Abi, and her mouth began to twitch. 'Catching tadpoles?' she said, bursting into laughter. 'That's a bed-warmer, you silly things! You put warm embers inside, closed it over, then stuck it between the sheets of the bed to warm it up before you got in.' She laughed again. 'Catching tadpoles,' she repeated, shaking her head as she left them to check on the other rooms.

From outside in the hall came the sound of girly laughter, high and silly. Then a voice said, 'Oh, Daniel, stop – you're *so* funny.' Chrissy. Elaine.

'You're *so* funny,' Grace mimicked, leering at Abi, who started to giggle.

Sarah walked through the door as Miss Flood left. 'Are any of the rooms soundproofed?' she asked as she came in. 'I need a barrier between my ears and Chrissy's voice.' She shook her head, her long red hair swinging from side to side. 'You do not want to see the way she's flirting with Daniel out there, or trying to flirt. And the poor guy looks like he wants the ground to open up and swallow him.'

'Poor Daniel.' Grace laughed. 'He'd be no match for her at all.'

Sarah looked around the room. 'Where's Hannah?'

Abi and Grace looked around too, puzzled. 'She was right there,' Abi said, pointing to the end of the room by the window.

Suddenly, they heard a muffled voice: 'I'm *mumble mumble* through *mumble mumble* . . . can't believe . . . *mumble mumble* . . .'

'Hannah?' Abi called cautiously. 'Is that you?'

'Of *mumble mumble* it's me.'

'We can't see you,' Abi said. 'Where are you?'

'This invisible voice thing is freaking me out, Hannah,' called Sarah.

Without warning, part of the wall popped out and a smiling Hannah emerged. The girls stared in disbelief as the wall silently fell back into place.

'How did you do that?' Grace demanded, working her way through the clutter to get to Hannah.

'I have died and gone to heaven,' Hannah announced dramatically. 'You will *not* believe what I've found.'

The girls pushed towards her, eager to see whatever it was she had stumbled on.

'What's in there?' Grace demanded impatiently. 'What did you find that was so exciting?'

Hannah took a deep breath. 'A writing room,' she said.

'Seriously?' said Sarah in disappointment. 'You had me thinking it was something actually interesting, Hannah. Just another room? Great, let's take out an ad in the paper, tell everyone.'

'But it's not just another room,' said Hannah, eyes shining. 'It's a small little room, with nothing but a beautiful old writing desk and chair in it and it feels . . . special. I can see why someone chose to write there. It has something . . . like an energy.'

The other girls looked at one another – only Hannah could be breathless about a writing room!

'So can you see the door?' she asked them.

Abi, Sarah and Grace stared at the wall. It was covered with a heavy velvet wallpaper and they couldn't see any lines to show a door frame.

'If I hadn't seen you come out of there,' said Grace, running her fingers along the wall, 'I'd say there was nothing here at all.'

Hannah grinned. 'I know. I found it by accident myself. I caught my foot on that box there and leant against the wall, and my elbow must have hit the button or whatever it is. It was about . . . here.' She pushed her hand against the wall, there was a soft *pop* sound and the hidden door sprang open.

'Crikey, that's good,' said Grace.

'Come on,' said Hannah. They pulled the door open and stepped through. On the other side was a small annex room. The only furniture was a stool, a lamp and a mahogany writing desk. Abi thought it felt cosy and hidden, like a secret world for one. There was a small vent at the top of one wall to let in fresh air, but otherwise it was a completely self-contained private room. As before, the door quietly fell back to become part of the wall.

Hannah looked besotted all over again. 'I'd love one of these,' she said, touching the polished surface of the writing desk. 'I think you could only write great things if you had a desk like this.'

'I've never seen a desk like that before,' Abi admitted. 'Does the front fold down?'

'Yes, it's got little drawers,' said Hannah. She folded down the front gently, revealing a series of small shelves and drawers. 'I suppose you put your paper here, pens and ink, all your bits and pieces. Then you leant on the folded-down desk to write.'

The girls opened the little drawers and nosied about in the hidey-holes in the bureau. Abi pulled open one drawer and stopped. 'Oh,' she gasped. 'There's something in here.' The others crowded closer to get a better look.

Abi tugged at the drawer, pulling it out as far as it would go. She put her hand in and could feel paper jammed at the back. She closed her fingers round it and pulled – whatever it was, it was stuck fast. She got a better grip and tugged again, harder this time. She could feel it giving way a little. One last tug and she yanked out . . . a small book. The girls stared at one another in delight.

'Oh wow,' said Hannah, 'something from the original owners. Wow!'

Abi looked at Hannah's rapt face and handed her the book. 'Here, Hannah, you read it.'

Hannah turned over the book and on the front, in elegant handwriting, was written:

Private Diary of Beryl Grainger

'Breathe, Hannah,' Sarah said, 'you look like you're going to faint with pleasure.'

She giggled. 'I am. I can't believe we've found something like this. How fabulous is that?'

'Open it,' Sarah said eagerly.

Hannah looked at her, shocked. 'I can't do that. It's private.'

Sarah stared at her. 'Hannah, the woman probably died years ago. I don't think she'd mind us having a look.'

Hannah looked uncertain. 'But . . . wasn't Beryl the name of the woman who last lived here? Remember, Mr Grainger said Beryl and Audoen were his parents, didn't he? So it's not that long ago. I can't open Simone's grandmother's diary.' She shook her head. 'It wouldn't be right.'

'I know what Hannah means,' Abi said uncertainly. 'It is a diary after all.'

'Give it to me, then,' Sarah said quickly, before Grace could agree with the others too. As Sarah reached for the book, Hannah took a step away from her and the book fell out of her hands and on to the floor. The pages fluttered open and the girls looked down and saw the words written there:

I have made two important discoveries: ghosts do not haunt, they are haunted; and I know how to help them. I am going to be a ghost detective.

They looked at one another, then back at the book. They could hear their own heartbeats in the silence. No one wanted to think about the mausoleum, or talk about it.

Finally, Sarah spoke: 'Good grief, Beryl was a mentaller.'

They all laughed nervously. 'What a strange thing to write,' Abi said. 'Do you think she really believed that stuff?'

'I'd like to refer you back to the mentaller point I made earlier,' Sarah said, like she was on the debating team. 'Ghost detective? *Seriously?* If she believed that, she had obviously spent too long locked up in this little room.'

'I don't know,' said Hannah. 'I mean, she mentions *discoveries*. That means something happened to convince her.'

Sarah looked impatient. 'Grace, back me up here. What would science say?'

Grace shrugged. 'My mother loves to tell me

that energy cannot be created . . . or destroyed. That would include people's energy, I suppose?'

'Grace, you're supposed to be a scientist,' Sarah protested. 'Girls, you're not really saying you believe in *ghost detectives*, are you? I mean, come on!'

'Well, I guess it is stretching things a bit far,' Abi conceded.

'Maybe,' Hannah said, 'Beryl was making notes for a novel she was planning to write? Maybe this isn't a diary in the sense we mean it?'

'That's true,' nodded Grace. 'We're just jumping to conclusions, aren't we?'

'Yeah, and I'm going to conclude old Beryl had a screw loose,' said Sarah, folding her arms. 'I mean, it's not like she had an Xbox or a Wii for entertainment. It's probably easy to make up this sort of stuff when you're half crazy with boredom.'

'That's what I love about you, Sarah,' Hannah said, shaking her head, 'your understanding for others.' She turned the book over in her hands. 'Perhaps we shouldn't put this on display in the museum,' she said.

'Why not?' asked Sarah. 'It's part of the house and the history of the owners.'

Hannah looked around the little room. 'Beryl obviously kept this place and this diary secret, so it seems wrong to suddenly put it out there for everyone to read . . . and probably laugh at her. I don't like the idea of it for her.'

Abi felt for Hannah – she obviously felt very strongly about protecting Beryl's privacy.

'Hannah,' said Sarah in disbelief, 'what's come over you? This is someone you don't know or care about. It's just another bit of the house.'

'I'm just saying –' Hannah began, but Abi shushed them. She had heard something.

Abi moved over to the hidden door and held her finger to her lips, motioning the others to be quiet. They could hear someone poking about in the drawing room, then saying to herself, 'Where *are* they?' Abi pointed at the door and mouthed one word: *Chrissy*. The girls froze, even Sarah. Whatever it was they had found and whether or not they decided to share it, there was no way anyone wanted Chrissy and her big mouth to get there before them. Abi didn't breathe as they listened to Chrissy working her way towards their doorway. Grace, Sarah and Hannah were perfectly silent, none of them moving an inch.

Chrissy stopped for a moment outside, then gave a frustrated sigh and moved off again. They could hear her expensive shoes click-clicking towards the drawing-room door.

Abi let out a long sigh of relief.

'We can't let her know about this place,' Hannah whispered. 'She'd run straight to Miss Flood to tell her and I just know Miss Flood would be so excited, she'd put the diary on display immediately. I say we need to think about it, at least for a little bit.' She stuffed the diary up her jumper, prepared to defend it at all costs.

Abi opened the door a crack. 'Coast's clear,' she said quietly, then slipped out noiselessly into the main room. She hurried to the closed door and stood guard while the other three crept out of the secret room and let the hidden door fasten shut behind them. Hannah had just stashed the diary safely in her backpack when the drawing-room door was flung open, and there stood Chrissy.

'Oh, very mature,' she said angrily, 'hiding from me when you know I've been sent to get you.'

'We weren't hiding,' said Grace. 'We were just . . . looking at something on the floor and . . . mustn't have heard you,' she finished weakly.

Chrissy narrowed her eyes and stared at her. 'The eighties called, Grace,' she said nastily, 'and they'd like their clothes back.' Grace didn't reply, just stuck her tongue out at her. 'Oh, wonderful response,' Chrissy snapped.

'What did you want, Chrissy?' Sarah asked quickly, trying to draw the fire away from Grace.

'Miss Flood wants us all in the sitting room. Now,' she said and stalked off.

'Don't listen to her,' Abi cried, when Chrissy had gone. 'You look fantastic, Grace, I think you always do.'

Grace smiled gratefully at her. 'Oh, don't worry about it, Abi, I'm used to her.'

'Come on,' Sarah said, 'we'd better get over there.' She looked back at the hidden door. 'We can decide what to do about the diary later.'

The four of them filed into the sitting room, where the other volunteers were sitting on the low sofas, pens and notebooks in hand.

'Now that we're *all* here,' Miss Flood began, shooting the four girls a pointed look, 'I'd like to do some forward planning.'

'Miss, when are we supposed to open as a museum?' Jack asked.

'Well, it's up to us really, although the sponsor, Miss Wells, isn't the easiest woman to deal with and I think she'll want to see progress soon enough. Let's try to figure out when we might be ready.'

They went through the work still to be done: a good clean-up everywhere, sorting out the furniture and objects and then setting them up in displays, with cards to explain them. The reception desk was already in place thanks to the council's efforts with the old museum, but there was still lots to be done. Miss Flood examined the list they had made. 'Looking at this,' she said, 'I'd say we'll need about eight weeks to get everything ready.'

Everyone agreed. It would take time, but the idea of re-opening a real museum – and working in it – was really exciting. All the hard work they were going to have to do over the coming weeks would be worth it.

Abi looked around the room at her fellow volunteers. She thought Chrissy and Elaine might have made more of an effort to look as excited as everyone else, but then she decided she couldn't think of *anything* that would persuade them to crack a genuine smile. Josh was sitting a little apart from the rest, which was his usual habit, but she could see a glint in his eyes. Even if he was a bit reserved, she could tell he shared their excitement at the idea of making this place work. Then there were her new friends, Hannah, Grace and Sarah. Abi was just so grateful she had met them and that they were getting to do this incredible project together. And now the house had shared one of its secrets with them, and only them. She felt like something really special was happening – even if she couldn't fathom what exactly it was just yet. One thing she felt sure of, though: time would tell.

7

At the Gate Lodge

The volunteers packed up their things and headed for the front door. Most of them had cycled to the Grainger house that day, except Josh, who was collected by his dad, and Chrissy. Her mother swept up the drive in a shiny black jeep, and Chrissy and Elaine ran off and jumped inside, without a backward glance. Abi, Grace, Sarah and Hannah walked down the driveway, pushing their bikes and chatting. As they approached the front gates, they could see lights on in the gate lodge. Hannah stopped walking and stood staring at the red-brick building.

'I've got it,' she said.

'Got what?' Abi asked, confused.

'What we have to do with the diary,' Hannah replied. 'We have to return it to the Graingers.'

'Mr Grainger?' Grace said.

Hannah turned to look at her friends. 'No, to Simone. It's her grandmother and . . .'

'. . . and it just seems right,' Abi finished for Hannah, smiling at her. 'I agree.'

Sarah and Grace looked at each other, torn between wanting to have more time with the diary and wanting to do the right thing. Abi understood how they felt – she felt the same way – but she could see that the two girls realized Hannah was right. It wasn't theirs to hold on to.

'Goodbye, Beryl,' Sarah muttered under her breath as they walked towards the undertakers' front door.

They rang the doorbell and Simone quickly answered the door. She blinked, not expecting to see the four girls standing there. 'Hi,' she said, 'what's up?'

'We need to talk to you,' Hannah said.

'Come on in,' Simone said, standing aside and letting them through. She led them into a sitting room with a fire blazing in a black stove. 'This is our private room,' she said to them. 'The families of our clients don't come in here.'

Simone settled into one of the armchairs, tucked her legs up under her and looked at them, waiting. The girls glanced at each other, unsure how to begin.

Now that she was presented with the perfect chance, Grace decided to be bold and ask what she had been wanting to ask since she first met Simone. 'I know you must get sick of people asking,' she said, 'but are you really . . . an undertaker?'

Simone smiled a little. 'Yes, I am. I used to work

here in my school holidays, but then a few years ago I convinced Dad to home-school me and let me work here properly, and that's working out really well for us. We live on the first floor and run the business from here.'

The girls were impressed – home-schooling and a family business sounded so grown up.

'That's just brilliant,' said Grace with a wide smile. 'You sound about three million times more interesting than any of us!'

'Speak for yourself!' Sarah said, pretending to be insulted.

Simone smiled at them. 'I don't really talk about it because people tend to think I must be a freak,' she said, 'but it's really interesting work. I have to talk to people at an awful time in their life, but it means that they're really honest, you know?'

'And what do you actually . . . do?' asked Abi with great curiosity.

'Well,' said Simone, taking a deep breath, 'I greet clients – living ones – when they come to visit their loved ones. I also help dress the bodies and I'm training at the moment in mortuary make-up.'

The girls stared at her, wide-eyed, trying to imagine pulling clothes on to heavy, cold, lifeless limbs. They couldn't. Simone looked around at them, aware of their silence and the thoughts that were keeping them silent. She looked self-conscious. She rubbed at her forehead, then shifted position in the armchair. 'Now,' she said, changing the subject, 'what did you want to say to me? Is it about the mausoleum?'

'Oh no,' Abi said quickly. 'That was just . . . a mistake. No, it's something else. It's about something we found up at the house.'

Hannah took over from Abi and began to describe how she had found the writing room and the desk and then how Abi had found the diary. She pulled it out of her bag and held it up. 'Beryl's your grandmother, isn't she?'

Simone nodded, never taking her eyes off the diary.

'We thought you might prefer to keep this private, rather than have it as part of the museum.' Hannah got up and put the diary into Simone's hands. 'And we haven't told anyone about the writing room either,' she said.

Simone turned the diary over in her hands. 'Beryl,' she whispered. She looked up at the girls again. 'Did you read it?' she asked sharply.

The girls looked at each other uncomfortably. 'No, we didn't open it,' Abi said carefully, 'but when I pulled it out of the bureau it fell open on the floor, so we saw some words on one page. But then we shut it again and haven't touched it since – only to bring it to you.'

Simone stared at her. 'And what words did you see written on the open page?' she asked, softer this time.

Abi cleared her throat. 'Well,' she began, 'it didn't make sense.' She looked around at her friends for help.

'We thought it might be notes for a novel,' Hannah said.

'Tell me,' Simone said.

Abi took a deep breath. 'It said she had made two important discoveries – that ghosts were haunted and that . . . she could help them.' She stared into the fire, not wanting to look at Simone. There was silence for a few moments; no one knew what to say.

'I suppose you've heard stories about Beryl?' Simone asked. They all shook their heads. 'Really?' she said. They shook their heads again.

'I'm surprised by that,' Simone said slowly, 'because the town people loved to spread the rumour that Beryl was a witch.'

'Well, if she was going about helping ghosts, I don't think she was doing herself any favours there,' Sarah said bluntly.

To their surprise, Simone laughed – it was the first time they'd heard her laugh properly.

'You're absolutely right,' she said finally. 'Beryl had no idea how eccentric she was and how much she freaked people out. She looked the lady of the manor, all pearls and designer clothes, but then she'd start talking about ghosts or something, and it would silence the room. The staff thought she was a bit crazy and that filtered out to the rest of the town. But she didn't care about any of them. I loved that about her.' Simone smiled to herself, lost in her own thoughts.

'Where does she live now?' Sarah asked. 'I'd say she'd get a laugh out of reading back over her diary.'

'She died when I was four,' Simone replied. 'But I remember her well and I still miss her. There was no one like Beryl, that's for sure.'

'But I'd say you've inherited some of her sassy attitude,' Grace said. 'You're not too bothered by people's ideas about you, are you?'

Simone smiled at her. 'No, I'm not, and I'd say that's something you and I might have in common.' Grace grinned back at her.

'And is Beryl buried down in the mausoleum?' Hannah asked.

'Yes, she died in 1999, so she was the last one laid to rest there. Dad and I will be next.'

Abi shivered at the idea. 'Can you tell us more about her ideas about the ghosts?'

'Do you believe in them?' Simone asked her.

'No . . . yes. Actually, I don't know,' Abi finished, flustered.

'I don't,' Sarah said firmly. 'This lot –' she jerked her thumb at her three friends – 'were a bit spooked when the diary fell open and they read those words, but I just thought Beryl must have had a screw loose.'

'*Sarah!*' Grace hissed.

Simone laughed again. 'It's fine,' she said to Grace. 'Don't worry about it. And besides, I agree with her.'

'You think your own granny had a screw loose?' Grace said, shocked.

'Well, no, but I think the whole ghost idea is nonsense. I spend every day with dead people and I've never seen anything. You'd think if there was such a thing as a ghost you'd find it hanging around a morgue. Wouldn't you?'

'I suppose so,' said Hannah, 'if they find it hard to leave this life.'

Simone shook her head. 'Beryl would have disagreed with that actually,' she said. 'She always said that ghosts weren't interested in this world, that they didn't notice the living at all.'

'What made her think that?' Hannah asked.

'Oh, it's a long story,' said Simone. 'I won't bore you with it.'

'Boring?' said Sarah. 'Seriously, Simone, can you picture anyone looking more interested than us?'

Simone looked around at their eager faces and smiled. Abi imagined that Simone probably wasn't used to having friends, but she hoped Simone realized that if anyone could appreciate Beryl's story, they could.

'All right,' she said, 'I'll tell you some of Beryl's story and what those discoveries were that she mentioned in the diary. She used to tell me about it when I was little, and she once told me that, when she wasn't here, her story would be in the diary for me to read. I had a look at it when I was about ten, but not since then.' She flicked through the diary, looking for the right pages. The girls waited.

Simone looked up at them and curled deeper into her chair. 'Beryl married my grandfather, Audoen, in 1956 and moved into the house. She loved the place and threw herself into managing it. She was walking through the house one day when she heard the sound of someone crying on the back stairs. She went over to find out who it was. When she got there, she saw a sort of hazy figure sitting on the steps, huddled up. As Beryl stood there trying to work out who it was, the figure threw back her head and wailed. It was a young woman, but she looked odd. Nothing specific, just a haziness about her – as if she wasn't coloured in properly, Beryl said. More like an outline than a full person. Beryl asked if she could help, but the young woman didn't answer. She was just wrapped up in grief, wailing and crying. Then, as Beryl stood there, watching, the figure started to shimmer and become more and more hazy, until she was gone.'

'Wow!' breathed Abi, totally caught up in the story. 'A ghost?'

'That's what Beryl thought,' Simone said, nodding. 'She became obsessed with finding out who the woman was and how to help her. She read everything she could get her hands on about the supernatural, but nothing told her what to do. She kept going back to the stairs and she saw the young woman a number of times, but she could never get her to talk to her.'

Simone opened the diary and thumbed the pages until she found what she was looking for. 'Here it is. Listen to this, Beryl wrote about what happened next.'

27 November 1956
I am really terribly distressed by the young ghost's plight. Today, I resolved to do everything in my power to break through her heart-wrenching grief and get her to hear and see me. So I assembled a number of items and waited at the back stairs. I heard the low wail first, then she slowly materialized before my eyes. I called out to her, but, as usual, she did not respond in any way – it was like shouting at a table or a chair. So I grabbed the heavy brass pot and wooden spoon I had filched from the kitchen and I banged with all my might, until my arm was sore with effort. It was to no avail; she didn't perceive me. I picked up a croquet ball and threw it past her. Again, nothing. I retrieved the ball and threw it again and repeated this for a few minutes, but she didn't flinch. I tried

scratching my nails down the wall in front of her, but that didn't work. I shook a rattle and I wrote out the word 'HELLO' on a large piece of white paper that I swished about in front of her face. Throughout all of these endeavours, she remained impassively locked in her own thoughts, whatever dreadful thoughts they may be. Finally, I tried what was likely a very silly approach – I draped myself in a white bed sheet and behaved in a ghostly fashion right in front of her. I had thought perhaps she would recognize 'her own kind', but it wasn't the case. I slumped down on the step beside her, spent, and we stayed that way for some minutes, until eventually the air shimmered around her and she was gone. I am quite at a loss as to what to do next.

Simone looked up from the diary. The four girls were listening intently. She smiled at them. 'I suppose you want to know if Beryl ever solved her ghost problem?'

'Oh, we're just a tiny bit curious,' Hannah said, making them all laugh.

Simone turned a couple of pages and stopped again. 'I'll let her tell you herself,' she said.

10 December 1956
Dearest, darling diary – a breakthrough! I am quite simply shaking with delight as I write this and recall all that has happened over the past twenty-four hours.

On Wednesday, Audoen announced that the following day he would have to attend a funeral in the next region, which meant an overnight stay. I am ashamed to say that I feigned a little turn, which ensured that I was considered to be in no fit state to accompany him. I had been busy hatching a plan in the last few days, trying to devise a way to finally reach out to my grief-stricken ghost. I had read a number of volumes on witchcraft and such like, and in the end I decided to create my own ritual, based on the various suggestions I had read. With Audoen out of the house, I could put my plan to work.

What I had decided was this: that the best way to attract her attention was to use beauty. Which of us can ignore beauty, after all? I determined that the greatest beauty in the world must be music because it can move us to tears. I had read much about the use of mirrors in these sorts of situations, so that seemed to make sense as well. And I thought a candle's flame would also prove a good attraction. A few minutes before midnight, I propped a mirror against the wall on the back stairs, then set a candlestick before it and lit the wick. The flame danced with its double in the mirror. Then I stood opposite the mirror, my back flattened against the wall, my violin in hand. As the clock struck midnight, I started to play Stravinsky's Concerto in D Major, a mournful, quite beautiful piece. I heard a rustling sound at my elbow, but I played on, eyes fixed firmly ahead. The air started to shimmer in that way with which I had become so familiar. Out of the corner of my eye, I saw her. She wasn't wailing. Her head was slightly to one side and I realized — good lord, she was listening! She drew closer, drawn by the music and the flame, and stepped into the space between me and the mirror, gazing intently at the flame. I hardly dared breathe, but held my ground and played on, watching her all the while. Then it was as if her eyes jumped into focus and she saw . . . me! She saw me behind her in the mirror. The poor thing nearly died all over again, such was the fright she got. Her eyes widened in terror and she dropped to her knees, calling on God to protect her. I actually burst out laughing, it was so terribly funny — a ghostly being wailing for protection from me! When she heard my laughter, she stopped praying and regarded me more closely.

After that, it was all quite easy. I explained to her that I was a living person, that I had been seeing and hearing her for some time. She in her turn explained that while she had known she was dead, she couldn't leave this place. It transpired that she had died in childbirth and she couldn't get over her grief for her baby, who had perished with her. Poor mites! She said she wished she could have named her baby, rather than have it die nameless. The baby had been a little girl, and she would have called her Hope. We talked for a time, and then she left with a sad little wave.

Well, I mulled it over all the next morning and realized I could do something about this. I consulted old Mr Grainger, Audoen's grandfather, and he recalled a young serving girl dying in this manner, giving her name as Wells. So off I went to the town graveyard and I read every tombstone in the place until I found what I was looking for: Mary Wells, 1920 – 1937. God took them as his own. RIP. *That was clue enough for me. I hurried back to Mr Grainger and asked him to release his head engraver for the afternoon, which he kindly did. Francis accompanied me to the graveyard and over the course of a few hours he added a name under Mary's:* Hope Wells.

That night, I waited eagerly for my ghost friend to appear, which she did. This time, she was immediately aware of me, so it seemed I had shifted things between us permanently. I asked her to meet me at the graveyard, and she agreed. I took a lamp, threw a cloak over my head and walked to the graveyard. Once there, I saw her waiting under a yew tree. I brought her to her own grave and stood aside to let her read the words engraved there. Oh, it was horrifying! She fell to her knees as if stabbed and emitted a sound that I really can't describe – a noise of pure grief. My own hands trembled to hear it and I felt tears coursing down my cheeks. She wept and wrung her hands, but slowly she became calmer. Eventually, she stood up and turned to face me. 'Thank you,' she said so quietly I strained to hear. Then she looked around and said, 'I am done here.'

With that, she disappeared. I know I won't see her again – I can feel it. That act freed her of the past, I think, and she has moved on to wherever the dead souls go.

I must admit to feeling completely changed by this whole extraordinary experience. The grief of that young woman was so profound, and yet it wasn't an eternal curse – I was able to help her. I feel such happiness that I could help her, and it makes me want to do more. Surely, there are many people who die with emotions and thoughts that will not let them rest?

Hannah whistled through her teeth. 'That is some story,' she said, falling back into her armchair.

'I really don't know what I think any more,' Abi said, shaking her head. 'I mean, that story, the details, could she really have imagined it?'

Simone looked over at Sarah. 'You're very quiet.'

Sarah slowly shook her head. 'I just can't accept it as real,' she said. 'Sure, it's a great story, but wailing ghosts? Midnight visits to tombstones? I don't know, it just seems a bit . . . makey-upy.' She looked at Simone. 'Do you know what happened after that? Did Beryl try to help others?'

'Yes.' Simone nodded. 'She perfected her ritual and used it as a siren call to any ghosts in need. What she said was that she had a natural feeling for this work, a special sensitivity to ghosts, which is why she saw the grieving ghost in the first place.'

At this, the four girls exchanged a quick look. Abi felt as if her blood was running cold in her veins. A natural feeling? A special sensitivity? Did that mean anyone who could see a ghost was special in some way? Her mind flitted back to the mausoleum. She had seen the girl in the white dress so plainly, and she kept wondering afterwards why it was only Hannah, Grace and Sarah who could see it too. The others and Simone were right there, but they saw nothing. Could it be that . . .? She shook her head, trying to shake out the thoughts that were taking root.

'So she decided to build on that,' Simone went on, 'and she said that for the rest of her life she was visited by ghosts and she helped them move on from whatever had caused them to get stuck in limbo. I remember her going to some houses in the town, places that were meant to be haunted and the families were at their wits' end. It was funny because everyone laughed at her, but when anything weird happened they came racing to the house for her help.'

'And what was her ritual to tell the ghosts she'd help them?' Grace asked.

Simone shrugged. 'It was just a mish-mash of ideas that she came up with herself, more or less as she described it in that last entry. It involved standing at a mirror . . . there was a song, I think

. . . hang on, it'll be in here.' She leafed through the diary, then read out a short passage:

I tried a few different variations, but after I did the following ritual the ghosts came through at their will. I stood at a mirror at midnight, and on the stroke of the clock I sang a song that I had written myself, to convey my intentions directly to the spirits. I had lit a white candle in front of the mirror. I also had a piece of white paper on which I had written 'I CAN HELP YOU', and I burned it in the candle's flame. It wasn't long after that that a ghost arrived, seeking my help.

'Does she give the lines of the song?' Grace asked. Abi looked at her – she seemed very interested to know the details of the ritual. Abi wasn't so sure that she wanted to know herself.

'Yes, they're here,' Simone replied. '*If you're filled with despair, lost and alone out there, I'm open to hearing your plight, I'd like to help you into the light.* To be sung to any jaunty air you please, it says underneath.' She smiled to herself. 'That's so Beryl.'

Sarah glanced at the clock on the wall. 'I have to get going,' she said, 'I've a piano lesson soon. Thanks for talking to us, Simone.'

Simone smiled. 'Thank you for this,' she said, rubbing the cover of the diary. 'I'm going to put it back in the vault, where it should have been.'

'Vault?' Hannah said, looking around. 'You have a vault?'

'Yep,' said Simone, 'in the basement. There's a special room with deposit boxes. It's very cool actually. People use them for personal effects or private messages they want to leave to someone, that sort of thing.' She patted the diary again. 'Beryl has her own box down there, so I'll return this to its rightful place. I've no idea how it ended up in the house.'

The girls began to gather their coats and bags. 'One more thing,' Simone said. 'Now that I've told you all that, would you mind telling me something?'

'Sure, what is it?' Grace asked.

'Well,' said Simone, looking down at her hands, 'Beryl never told me about the writing room. Would you mind showing it to me some day?'

'She never showed you?' Sarah said. 'Why not? She told you all about ghosts and things.'

Simone shrugged. 'I don't know why not. I guess she just wanted it for herself. But I'd love to see it.'

'Of course we'll show you,' Sarah said, 'but we'll have to be sneaky about it so the others don't all follow us.'

'We'll figure out something,' Abi promised her, 'and get you into it as soon as we can.'

The four girls said goodbye to Simone and headed outside and into the misty evening air that was pressing against the gate lodge. Simone stood staring after them for a few moments, then threw a log on the fire and settled down to read her grandmother's diary.

8

The Summons

The girls cycled home quickly, so Sarah wouldn't be late for her lesson. Abi noticed that they all looked preoccupied, lost in thought about Beryl's story. When they reached the gates of Sarah's house, Grace suddenly spoke up. 'Let's get together later. Can you all get out to my place?'

'I'm babysitting my pain of a little brother tonight after my lesson,' Sarah said gloomily.

'Would it be all right if we all called into you then?' asked Grace.

'Yeah, I suppose so,' said Sarah, frowning, 'but what for? What's on your mind?'

Grace ignored her question. 'Shall we say Sarah's place at half eight?' she asked. Hannah glanced at Abi and raised her eyebrows. *What's Grace up to?* Abi wondered.

'See you later,' Grace called over her shoulder as she shot off. The others looked at one another.

'What's with her?' Sarah asked.

'I've no idea,' Hannah said. 'I guess we'll find out later.'

They said goodbye and Sarah went into her house to meet her piano teacher while Hannah and Abi went their separate ways.

For the next three and a half hours, Abi barely heard anything her parents said to her – she was miles away, back in the Grainger house with Beryl, wondering about everything. It was all she could think about.

Abi's mum was happy to let her go out to Sarah's house, delighted that she had made friends at last. Abi kept glancing up at the clock, willing the hands to move quicker so she could see the girls again and talk it all over. Eventually, the clock said 8:15 and she grabbed her coat and shouted a hasty goodbye to her parents. The night was damply cold and Abi buried her chin into her scarf as she walked round to Sarah's house and rang the bell.

Sarah led her into the kitchen, where Hannah was already sitting, looking as impatient as Abi felt. The doorbell rang again and Sarah went out to let Grace in.

Grace came into the kitchen, rosy-cheeked from the cold, her many bangles jangling and a hippy-style tote bag slung over her shoulder. It was covered with beads and mirrors and made Abi think of pictures she'd seen of cool music festivals. Where Grace had managed to get her hands on it, she could only imagine.

'Right,' Grace said, 'I have a suggestion to make and I want you all to keep an open mind about it.'

'Hang on,' interrupted Sarah. 'Let me just check where Aaron is. He'll be doing his best to spy on us, no doubt.' She flung open the kitchen door and bellowed, 'Aaron? Where are you?'

'Xbox,' came the muffled reply.

'Good, he's in the den. He won't be able to hear anything from there. Go on, Grace,' she said, 'what's this suggestion?'

'I want to do an experiment and I need your help,' said Grace, opening her bag.

'Science again, Grace?' said Hannah. 'Is now the time . . .' Her voice trailed off as she saw what Grace was pulling out of the bag: white candles and bits of paper. 'What are they for?' Hannah asked slowly, glancing nervously at Abi and Sarah.

Grace took a deep breath and looked at her friends. 'I want us all to do Beryl's ritual.'

'Seriously?' Sarah demanded in disbelief. 'Why?'

'Well,' said Grace, 'us three don't know what to believe and you're sure it's nonsense, so I thought it would be interesting to do it and see if anything happens. If nothing happens, it's all "baloney", as Abi would say, but if something does happen . . .'

'If something happens, what?' Sarah said. 'We get stuck in limbo with a bunch of unhappy dead people?'

'But, Sarah,' said Grace, grinning at her, 'you're the one who doesn't believe in any of this, so you should be looking forward to doing it, to prove that being a ghost detective is a stupid idea.'

Sarah bit her lip. 'It's just a creepy waste of time,' she complained.

Abi was surprised – Sarah looked about as nervous as she felt. She thought straight-shooting Sarah would have been game for something like this.

'Well, that's exactly what we're going to prove,' Grace said, sounding determined. 'We need to know, otherwise none of us will ever stop thinking about it. Agreed?' she asked, looking round at the three girls.

Grace was right, Abi decided. At least this way they'd know for sure if what Beryl wrote was just a fantasy, or something more. She nodded her agreement.

Hannah gave a lopsided smile. 'Let's do it.'

'Well, if everyone's doing it then I suppose I have to join in too,' Sarah huffed.

Abi grinned. Sarah looked more curious now than she was letting on.

'Right, I have a white candle each and I've got four slips of paper here with the words "I CAN HELP

YOU" written on them, like Beryl did. So now we just have to pick a tune for the song, then we can synchronize our watches to make sure in our houses tonight we all do the ritual at midnight on the dot.'

Abi got a fit of the giggles. 'All right, James Bond, let's *synchronize our watches*,' she teased. Hannah and Sarah started giggling too, and soon all four of them were doubled over laughing. They didn't hear the kitchen door being pushed open or see Aaron standing there, staring at them with his mouth open.

'What's got into you lot?' he demanded.

Sarah wiped tears from her eyes. 'Nothing. What do you want?'

'Juice,' he said, still staring at them. 'What are you doing with those candles?'

'Mind your own business,' Sarah warned.

'Weirdos,' he muttered under his breath.

'Here's your juice,' Sarah said, handing the carton to him. 'Back to the Xbox with you.'

As he left the room, he called back, 'All you need is a cauldron and pointy hats and you'd look like crazy witches.'

Hannah raised an eyebrow at Grace. 'See, we haven't even done the silly ritual yet and already we're being called witches. Are you sure you want to do this?'

'Yes,' said Grace firmly. 'Come on, Sarah, give us a tune for the words.'

They went into the small music room next door and Sarah bashed around on the piano until she found something that worked. They practised singing the words until they all had it. They went back into the kitchen and Grace started handing round the candles and paper. 'Now, you'll have to set up in front of a mirror, remember, and sing while staring at your own reflection. Do you all solemnly swear to do it? I don't want anyone lying and saying they did it when they didn't.'

'Well, that's the end of my cunning plan,' Abi declared and they all dissolved into giggles again.

'Come on,' said Grace, 'swear on something that you'll do it.'

Abi assumed a solemn air and raised her right hand. 'I swear on Beryl's diary that I will perform the ritual at midnight.'

'That'll do,' said Grace with a smile. 'Now you, Hannah.' Hannah raised her right hand and repeated the vow. 'Sarah?' Grace said. Sarah looked for a moment like she might say *no*, but then she sighed and raised her right hand and swore the oath too.

'Fantastic,' said Grace, beaming at them. 'This will be really interesting. Now, get out your mobiles and we'll set the clocks to the exact same time.'

Just before midnight, in four houses across the town, candle flames flickered against the indifferent surfaces of four mirrors. In front of each mirror stood a girl, holding a piece of paper and a mobile phone as she counted down the seconds to 00:00. As the numbers flicked to exactly midnight, four mouths opened and the sweet sound of an old song fluttered out into the night air:

> '*If you're filled with despair,*
> *lost and alone out there,*
> *I'm open to hearing your plight,*
> *I'd like to help you into the light.*'

Four hands reached out towards the flames and allowed the pieces of paper to crease and burn, until nothing remained. In the silence that followed, the stars and moon became slightly blurred as the night air over the town shimmered, then settled back into place. Three phones vibrated in their owners' hands.

> I'm sure that qualifies us as mentallers too!
> Goodnight x

9

The Visit

All that week in school, Abi and the girls gathered together first thing in the morning, before class had started, to find out if anyone had seen anything. Every morning it was the same: the four friends looked at each other with a silent question, then shook their heads, feeling a bit relieved and a bit disappointed at the same time. They had done the ritual, just like Beryl described it, but nothing had happened. Abi felt mostly relieved as ghosts were always a scary prospect, but she felt sad too. Beryl had been able to help so much and do so much good, but it looked like she and her new friends wouldn't be able to do the same. She found herself constantly remembering back to the moment in the mausoleum when she had seen the girl in the white dress and felt a deathly shiver through her bones. There *was* something there, she just knew it. Was it someone who needed help? Now she'd never know.

*   *   *

Friday, after school, the girls came to Abi's house to hang out. She had decided to introduce her friends to a little bit of America and make chocolate-chip cookies for them. She could tell that her mom and dad were thrilled to see Hannah, Sarah and Grace arriving at the house. The four girls had become such a unit over the past few weeks, always laughing and joking around. Her parents smiled widely as they ushered the girls into the kitchen to join her, then shut the door to give them time alone.

'I think we can safely say that *I* was right,' Sarah said with a grin, as the four girls sat round the kitchen table, taking it in turns to lick the spoon of cookie dough. I can't believe you all fell for the idea of being ghost detectives! Beryl was just lonely and bored and she made up stories to amuse herself. Didn't she?' she demanded.

'I'm glad we tried it, all the same,' Grace said. 'Now at least we know for sure.'

'I know. I feel a bit sad about it all for some reason though,' Hannah said. 'We could have been part of Beryl's story.'

'Book geek,' Sarah teased.

'Just hand back the cookie-dough spoon,' Hannah ordered, laughing.

'So now that we don't have to talk about being ghost detectives all the time, let's talk about you, Abi! What do you think of the place now?' Sarah asked. 'Do you like the school, the people?'

Abi shifted uncomfortably as the attention focused on her, and Grace and Hannah looked up, interested to hear what she would say.

'Oh yeah,' Abi said, nodding her head. 'I'm so glad I've met you, Grace and Hannah, you're all awesome.'

'We do try,' Sarah said solemnly, as the others burst out laughing.

'School is pretty much OK,' Abi went on. 'I find the teachers easy to talk to and most of the kids. The best bit has to be the museum though. I'd never have pictured working in a place like that, ever.'

'I know how you feel,' Hannah said quietly. 'I love reading and hanging out with you girls, but the museum feels like something else. Something . . . I don't know . . . maybe life-changing?'

Abi looked at her thoughtfully and Grace nodded in agreement. 'Yeah, that's how I feel,' Grace said, pushing her hair back from her forehead with her arm. 'I can't explain it, but it feels like something we're meant to do, you know?'

Sarah's face broke into a mischievous grin. 'And what about the boys?' she said.

Abi blushed and looked away. 'Oh, they're all lovely guys.'

'Is any one of them more lovely than the rest?' Sarah persisted, twirling a strand of her long red hair innocently round her finger.

Abi shook her head vigorously. 'Oh no,' she said, 'they're all . . . fine.' Josh was the only boy she really thought about from the museum and she wasn't even really sure why she did – he always seemed so serious and moody. It wasn't a feeling she could explain to the girls, so Abi decided to keep it to herself for the moment.

'Never mind Abi's choice in boys, Sarah.' Grace came to her rescue. 'What about Daniel Binoche, the hottest half-French boy in a ten-mile radius?'

Sarah blushed in a most un-Sarah-like way. 'Oh well, I don't know. I know that Chrissy trails after him *all* the time. And she always ends up with boys having crushes on her.'

'Yes, well,' said Hannah, in a very dodgy American accent as she handed Sarah back the spoon and the bowl. 'What Chrissy doesn't have is chocolate coooookies!'

The girls whooped with laughter.

Sarah eagerly dipped in and tasted a bit, closing her eyes and sighing. 'Now that . . . is seriously good,' she said.

The next morning, Abi arrived at the Grainger house with a box of cookies tucked under her arm and invited everyone to dig in. She had made extra so the rest of the volunteers could enjoy a bit of America too.

'Did you make these?' Jack asked, cookie crumbs sticking all over his freckly face.

'We all did,' Abi replied, smiling at her three new friends.

'Losers,' they heard Elaine mutter.

'Are you enjoying that cookie, Elaine?' Sarah said sweetly. Elaine made a face at her and then she and Chrissy took their cookies to the other side of the room and sat with their heads bent together, whispering and giggling.

'Don't mind them,' Daniel said. 'These cookies are amazing.'

'Thanks,' Sarah said, handing him another. Abi grinned at the others.

'Thanks, Abi,' Josh said, brushing crumbs off his sweater. 'I'm going back to look at those speakers now.'

'Oh, you're welco–' Abi began, but Josh had already gone.

Abi saw Hannah watching her and blushed. To her relief, Hannah didn't say anything in front of the others but just gave Abi's arm a squeeze.

'I'll go with him,' Daniel said, smiling at Josh's abruptness. 'Thanks again for the cookies!'

Hot on Daniel's heels, Chrissy and Elaine walked out without thanking the girls, but grabbing the last two cookies on the way.

Abi was just about to say something to them

when Grace's head snapped up. 'What did you say?' she asked.

'I didn't say anything yet, Grace,' Abi replied, confused.

Grace whipped round to look at Hannah and Sarah. They shook their heads. 'Not us either,' Hannah said.

'Oh,' said Grace, frowning, clearly puzzled about something. 'Let's get back to the schoolroom and carry on sorting the stuff there, then.'

They all turned to walk towards the door and back to work, when Grace suddenly stopped dead in her tracks. 'Come on, that's not funny,' she said. 'Which one of you is saying that?'

The rest of them looked at her astonishment. 'Er, Grace,' Sarah said with a tight smile, 'we've moved on from the spooky ghost-detecting, so it's really not helpful to start freaking us out all over again. No one said anything, OK.'

Grace looked at them suspiciously. 'OK,' she said, but not sounding at all convinced.

Abi was starting to feel nervous. There was something about Grace's face that reminded her of how she had looked in the mausoleum.

They moved towards the door again, but this time it was Hannah who stopped in her tracks.

'Oh, for goodness' sake,' Sarah began, but then she stopped. Raising her arm slowly, she pointed in the same direction that Hannah was looking.

Abi and Grace followed her line of view up to the window.

Beyond the glass, the air was shimmering – like a patch of air they couldn't quite see through. But that wasn't all.

She was there! The girl in white from the mausoleum was at the window, staring hard at them. Abi felt the breath stop in her chest. She gasped. It was the same girl – she was still wearing the lace dress and veil and still holding her withered flowers and piece of paper. This time, she wasn't crying. She was looking directly at them, intently. Slowly, her lips parted and softly, so softly, she spoke. She said just two words: 'Help me!'

Without a word between them, the girls turned and charged out of the door, across the reception area, into the drawing room and across to the hidden door of the writing room. Hannah banged the wall, the door popped open and they all scrambled to get inside, to hide from the dreadful vision lurking at the window.

10

The Bride's Story

'OK, I'll go first,' said Sarah. '*What was that?*' Her voice was high and she sounded very scared.

'I saw the girl in the white dress with the veil and holding the same piece of paper,' Abi replied shakily. 'Is that what you all saw?' They nodded, their hearts beating wildly at the thought of it.

'She's out of the mausoleum,' Grace whispered, her eyes wide with fright.

'I really thought I was seeing things,' Hannah said quietly, 'but then I heard the words, *Help me*, and I nearly peed in my pants.'

'Was that really . . . a ghost?' Grace asked.

'Well,' said Sarah, 'she was deathly pale, unmoving and unblinking and seemed to be able to talk almost by telepathy. I think "ghost" just about covers it. Besides, you of all people should know.'

'What do you mean?' Grace said nervously.

'Well, *you* insisted we do the ritual and *you* gave us candles and everything, and now *you* seem surprised that we have actually called up the dead!'

'But I didn't think it would *work*!' cried Grace. 'I thought it would just show us that ghosts *weren't* real.'

'Oh, Grace,' Hannah said softly, but with real disappointment in her voice.

'Welcome to the world of the scientific experiment,' Sarah said sharply. 'Results can go one way or the other. We told you that!'

Grace looked like she might cry, and Abi immediately wrapped her arm round her and turned on the other two. She couldn't stand to see her friends fighting. 'Leave her alone,' she said angrily. 'Grace thought it was a bit of fun and we agreed to do it, so we can't blame her now.' Sarah and Hannah stared down at their feet, ashamed of picking on Grace.

'Sorry,' Sarah muttered, 'I'm just so freaked out.'

'We need to figure this out,' Abi said firmly. 'We did a ritual last week that was meant to let ghosts know they can come to us for help, right?'

'Right,' they all agreed.

'Well, it's not really the ghost's problem if we're scared. We did it and, if this really is a ghost, it's turned up because it needs help – and we said we'd help. We saw her that day in the mausoleum, even if we didn't admit it, and then we went on to do the ritual, basically telling her we could help. That's our fault, not hers.'

Sarah looked at her in disbelief. 'Abi, are you saying what I think you're saying? That we have to look for this thing and try to . . . *talk to it?*'

'Yes,' Abi said stubbornly. 'You can't say you'll help, then run away when someone asks for help.'

'You want us to go back out there and look for her?' Grace said, sounding like she'd rather dance naked into the classroom on Monday – or, even worse, wear normal clothes. Abi opened her mouth to speak, but someone got there before her.

'There you are!'

The girls spun round and looked at the door – who had found the writing room? It was a girl's voice, but it didn't sound like Chrissy or Elaine. They pressed their ears against the wall, straining to make out who was on the other side. The voice spoke again. 'Whatever are you doing? That is the queerest behaviour I have ever seen.'

The girls were motionless. The voice was *inside* the writing room. Slowly, they moved their heads away from the wall and turned round. The girl in the white dress was sitting on the stool at the bureau, the air around her shimmering as it had at the window. Four mouths fell open, but no sound emerged. The girls reached for each other and stood in a row before the ghost, hands held, eyes wide, like a string of crazy paper dolls.

As they continued to stand there, unmoving, the ghost eventually gave a little laugh and waved her hand in front of them. 'Hello? Is anyone there?' she called, before dissolving into laughter at her own joke. Abi took a deep breath, cleared her throat a little, then took one step forward. She was the one who had persuaded the girls that they had to help the ghost, so she knew she should be brave enough to speak to her first.

'Hello.' Abi's voice faltered slightly. 'Who . . . who are you?'

'First of all,' said the girl in a cold voice, 'I need to establish who *you* are. Are you, in fact, a ghost detective?'

Abi gulped. 'Well . . . sort of,' she managed to say, in a weak voice.

The ghost narrowed her eyes. 'Has the cat got your tongue, miss?' she demanded. 'Are you or are you not able to help me?'

Abi thought her heart was going to beat right out of her chest. Then, just at the worst moment, she had a flash of Hannah saying she'd nearly peed her pants and she could feel a giggle rising in her chest. She started to feel slightly hysterical – something that always happened when she was scared. The giggle rose even higher. *Oh no*, she thought to herself, *don't let me laugh now*. She struggled to swallow it back down, but fear and hysteria were mingling in an explosive mix. She looked at the ghostly figure and opened her mouth to say that she *was* a ghost detective, but all that came out was a snort of laughter. The other girls looked at her in shock.

The girl in the white dress stared disdainfully at Abi. 'I think,' the ghost said primly, 'I shall try directing my question to someone else.'

Abi was mortified. She hoped her friends would understand. 'I'm so sorry,' she said in a strangled whisper, before clamping her hand to her mouth again.

The ghost turned to fix her stare on Hannah. 'You,' she said, 'can you help me?'

Hannah's head swivelled from the stricken Abi to the snippy ghost. She gulped and said in a small voice, 'Yes, I think we can. We can try.'

The ghost didn't seem impressed with this answer. 'Did you announce your intentions to help?' she asked impatiently.

This time Hannah nodded quickly. 'Yes, we did,' she said, speaking more strongly now. Abi was really proud of her friend. 'We performed the ritual,' Hannah continued, 'and if you are in distress, we will do our best to help.'

The ghost seemed mollified by this. She shifted on the seat and her dress rustled faintly. Abi looked at her properly for the first time. She had long black hair, which was caught back loosely under her lace veil, and her eyes looked like they might be grey, but it was hard to tell – they shifted colour with the light. She was slim, with very fine long fingers that looked like they would play a piano well, like Sarah's. Her dress was of lace and very simple but elegant – covering her shoulders, with long tight sleeves and a lace bodice. She looked young and very pretty. Her hands still clutched the dead posy and the piece of paper.

This time Grace stepped forward. 'Your dress is wonderful,' she said quietly. 'Is it vintage lace?'

The girl in the white dress smiled a little for the first time. 'Thank you, I made it myself.' She looked unbearably sad. 'The lace was cut from my mother's wedding train,' she said softly. 'I wanted to share a wedding dress with her.'

'Oh,' said Grace, 'it is a wedding dress, then? You look so young, I thought it couldn't be.'

'Yes, it's my wedding dress,' said the girl. She bent her head and began to cry. The four girls immediately tried to comfort her, forgetting they had been terrified of her until now.

'Oh, don't cry,' whispered Grace. 'We'll help you.'

Abi had recovered herself by now and she moved closer to the girl, kneeling down in front of her. 'It's OK,' she said gently. 'You're not alone.'

The ghost raised her head and looked at them gratefully. 'No one has said words like that to me in a long, long time,' she sniffed.

'Why don't you tell us why you're here,' said Hannah, 'then we might be able to help you.' The four girls sat down on the floor around the stool and the ghost started to tell them her story.

'My name is Louise-Anne Miller. I was born in this town in 1870. I am here because of this letter,' she said, clutching the paper to her chest, 'which has trapped my heart. My father was anxious for me to be wed as soon as I turned sixteen, and he searched for the right suitor. He presented two gentlemen to me, but I couldn't have married them. They were much older than me and we shared nothing in common. But the real reason was that . . . I was in love with Henry Grainger.' Her voice caught on his name and she started to cry quietly again.

'Did he know Beryl?' Abi whispered.

'I'm not aware of a Beryl Grainger,' she said with a frown. 'Henry was Celia's eldest son. He had one brother, Charles, to whom he was devoted and a sister, Lilian, and Celia was devoted to all of them.'

'So who did you marry?' Sarah asked.

'No one,' the ghost wailed, and sobbed again.

'Oh, sorry,' said Sarah, looking embarrassed. Hannah glared at her. Sarah mimed zipping up her mouth and throwing away the key.

Louise-Anne composed herself again and they all listened intently. 'Forgive me,' she said, 'it is so hard to speak of these things. Henry broke my heart and I have spent all this time lost in my grief, not knowing what happened. I don't believe what it says in the letter,' she said, looking earnestly at them, 'so I can't rest. I don't believe it's the truth, but what is?'

'Start at the beginning,' Hannah said gently.

'Celia was a very kind woman. Although my father was only a merchant, when she realized that I loved gardening, she invited me to see her garden, behind the house. My father seemed agitated by this, but he did not prevent me visiting Celia. As we walked about the place that first day, we were joined by Henry. He later told me he had seen us from an upstairs window and came racing down to find out who I was.' She smiled at the memory. 'Every week that summer I visited the garden and Henry would always find an excuse to talk to me. One day, I dropped my handkerchief on the path. I knew he had seen me drop it, so he ought to have returned it to me. But he didn't. I knew then that he felt more for me than passing friendship.'

The girls looked at one another in confusion. 'You dropped a hanky and he didn't give it back and that meant . . . love?' Grace asked.

Abi felt as confused as Grace sounded and she waited for Louise-Anne to explain.

'Well, yes, of course,' Louise-Anne replied in surprise. She looked at their faces. 'He kept it,' she said emphatically. The girls exchanged a silent look and nodded at her to go on.

'Then one day I left my parasol on a bench while I helped with some pruning and, when I returned to fetch it, there was a book of poetry placed beside it. The sonnets of William Shakespeare. Inside was an inscription dedicating the book to me, and I cherished it. Now I knew he loved me. On the first of October, Henry proposed to me. We were seated in the drawing room and his mother went out of the room to greet a visitor, leaving us alone for a few minutes. He crossed the room quickly, dropped to one knee and asked me to be his wife. I said yes, then I had to contain my emotions while his mother ushered in an elderly aunt and we discussed trivial things for the next hour. It was an exquisite torture, to be so near him and knowing what had passed between us but unable to look at him as I wished to.'

'So what happened?' asked Abi. 'If you loved each other and you were engaged to be married, what went wrong?'

Louise-Anne sighed and a cold breeze shivered across the girls' skin, giving them goosebumps. Abi realized that this was what she had felt in the mausoleum. Louise-Anne had been there all along. She knew it.

'It was difficult,' Louise-Anne said quietly. 'We knew our parents would be shocked, but we were not prepared for my father's reaction. He forbade me to marry Henry. He said the Graingers were not like us, that I could not marry into such a family. I did not know, but he had nursed a long-standing feud with one of the old Graingers and had a hatred in his heart for the whole family. I was inconsolable. A few days later, as I was walking on the lane near my home, a horse galloped up and Charles Grainger, Henry's brother, dismounted. He was a charming fellow, although a bit of a cad, by all accounts. He quickly told me that Henry wished to marry me still and had sent him to ask if I would be willing to elope and wed in secret.'

Hannah couldn't help herself, she gasped. The idea of running away to marry was so romantic! Abi smiled over at her.

'I agreed. I no longer cared what my father said or thought. I was so disappointed in him, putting an old feud over my happiness. He had not acted in a very fatherly manner, so I resolved not to act in a very daughterly manner. Charles hastily told me the plan: on the Eve of All Souls, when the town would be noisy with festivities and my father would be busy with his trade, I was to steal away to a town eight miles distant, in the next parish. Henry would be waiting for me. The priest there had agreed to perform the rites, and we would wed at six of the morning, before the cock crowed. We could then return to the town as man and wife, and my father would be powerless to prevent it. I gave him my word and Charles galloped away to inform Henry.'

'Eve of All Souls is Hallowe'en, isn't it?' Hannah asked. 'The last day of October?'

'Wow, you made your dress so fast!' Grace marvelled. 'You must have had only about three weeks to do it?'

'Yes,' Louise-Anne said with a smile. 'I worked late into the night, my eyes straining by the meagre light of the oil lamp, sewing and sewing until my fingers were sore. But nothing mattered, only that I marry Henry. I was so happy.'

Abi saw Hannah blinking hard. She was obviously trying to stop the tears that were threatening to spill over. 'What happened on the night you were meant to marry?' Abi asked the ghost.

'That is the part of the story that I do not fully know,' Louise-Anne said sadly. 'I dressed for my wedding and threw a long cloak over my head, fastening it at the chest to hide the dress. I slipped out of the house at three o'clock, unnoticed, and walked all the way to the church, in the darkness. I was frightened, but I had to keep going. I reached the church at a quarter before six. It was set back from the village road and surrounded by a thicket of trees. I mused that Henry had chosen well for our purposes. I pushed open the door. There were candles lit in niches along the wall and the smell of incense lingered. I crept up the aisle as quiet as a mouse and made my way to the sacristy. The priest was there and greeted me warmly. There was no sign of Henry. We waited, watching the minutes tick past. Finally, at half past eight we heard the dull thud of hooves approaching. I hid in the sacristy and the priest waited in the nave. The rider entered the church. He walked straight up to the priest, handed him a letter and said, "See that the young miss gets that." Then he left. The priest handed me the letter. I opened it and read the words written there: "*I cannot marry you. I am deeply sorry that I misled you. H. G.*" Those words are engraved on my heart.' She started to sob again.

'Oh my goodness, that's terrible!' Abi couldn't imagine the heartache Louise-Anne must have felt.

'So, do you want us to get revenge on Henry in some way?' Sarah asked.

The ghost looked shocked and the girls felt the goosebumps rise on their skin again. 'Certainly not,' she said in annoyance. 'Haven't you listened to anything I've said? Henry loved me,' she said, twisting the letter in her hands. 'I want you to help me by finding out *why* he didn't meet me. Something had to have kept him from me. I simply don't believe that he changed his mind. It's not possible.'

'But you didn't actually know each other very well,' Sarah said. 'A few turns around the garden and a dropped hanky don't really mean that much, do they?'

'Nice one, Sarah,' mumbled Grace. 'Super-sensitive, as always.'

But it was too late. The air around Louise-Anne was starting to shimmer and her eyes flashed with anger. 'How dare you!' the ghost shrieked. 'I *knew* Henry and he loved me!'

'It's OK,' said Abi soothingly. 'Louise-Anne, what else can you tell us about what happened afterwards? Did Henry ever contact you again? Or Charles? Do you know where Henry went?'

The ghost looked at Abi. 'I've no idea,' she said, 'because I died two days later.'

'Oh,' said Abi, shocked. 'But you were only sixteen?'

The ghost sighed. 'I had no choice but to make my way home again. I walked eight miles through rain and wind, not caring about anything, broken inside. By the time I reached home I was feverish. I was put to bed and the doctor was called, but he was too late. Since then, I have been in the mausoleum where you found me. For some reason, I have not been able to leave it – until now.'

The girls glanced at each other, each one thinking the same thing: *How on earth do we help her?* Before they could say anything, they heard their names being called from somewhere.

'Shoot,' said Abi, glancing at the door, 'it's our teacher. We have to go,' she added, turning to Louise-Anne, 'but we will try to help you. We just need some time to figure out what we can do.'

The ghost bride smiled sadly. 'Time is something I have plenty of,' she replied.

'We'll talk again soon,' Abi whispered. 'Goodbye for now.'

The girls sneaked out through the hidden door and tried to look busy in different parts of the room. They were just in time. The drawing-room door opened and Miss Flood poked her head in. 'Oh, there you are,' she said. 'We're all getting ready to leave, so finish off what you're doing.'

'Yes, Miss,' they called. 'On our way.'

11

The First Clue

The girls were anxious to see each other on Sunday and talk about everything that had happened, but Hannah had a tennis match to play, Sarah said something about having to do something with her parents at home, and Grace and Abi were dragged out on family trips. As it was a school night, their parents wouldn't let them get together on Sunday evening. It was maddening – more had happened in one day than had ever happened in their lives before, and they couldn't talk about it! Abi sent round a text message suggesting they get to school early, so they could talk before class started.

Finally, it was Monday morning. The girls were at the school at 8.15, surprising the caretaker when he came down to unlock the gate. They rushed past him and straight into the cloakroom, throwing down their bags and gathering in a tight huddle on the bench.

'Did anyone get any sleep at all this weekend?'

Abi asked. Her friends smiled and shook their heads.

'I even lost my match yesterday because I couldn't concentrate on the ball,' Hannah said, shaking her head.

'I felt like breaking out of the house last night and climbing in your bedroom windows,' Grace said. 'I thought I was going to burst if I didn't talk about it.'

'Now that really would have made me feel like I was in a movie,' Sarah said, laughing.

'What, you mean you don't climb into bedroom windows every night in this town?' Abi teased, as the others laughed. 'But really though,' Abi said, looking worried again, 'what are everyone's thoughts about what happened on Saturday?' They glanced at each other: where to begin?

'That was the craziest day ever,' Grace said. 'I never thought I'd meet a real live ghost, if you know what I mean. When I saw her at that window . . .' She trailed off, shaking her head in wonder.

'And you, Abi,' Sarah said with a grin, 'laughing at her!'

Abi blushed. 'Don't remind me,' she groaned. 'I just couldn't help thinking about Hannah peeing her pants and then I was so terrified as well, and it all just came out as a laugh.'

Her friends laughed. 'It was so funny,' Grace wheezed.

'It's a pity Beryl didn't send a ghost detective manual along with the diary,' Hannah said. 'It would have been good to have some idea how you talk to a ghost.'

They fell quiet, realizing how quickly they had started to talk about ghosts and ghost detecting as if they were normal things. Abi thought about how her mother always talked of not burning your bridges in life – now, she felt like a bridge had burned behind her and she could never go back to the Abi she had been before Saturday. Everything was different.

'So it really was real?' Sarah asked quietly.

'Yes,' Grace said firmly, 'it was. And now we've got a big problem to solve – how do we find out about Henry Grainger?'

'Well, I told my dad I wanted to look up the history of the Grainger family,' Hannah said, 'and he said the best place to look would be the parish records office. But it only opens on Saturday, from ten to four.'

'Where is it?' asked Abi.

'In an office in the town library,' Grace replied.

'What can we do before then?' Hannah asked. 'I wish I could get into the library at the museum; I'm sure I could dig up something there, but I have to wait until Saturday for that too.'

They were quiet for a moment, then Sarah shouted, 'Of course! It's easy!'

Abi jumped in her seat and Grace and Hannah

looked at Sarah in shock. 'Careful with the loud noises there, Sarah,' Grace said. 'Remember, we're all feeling a little bit spooked!'

'Sorry,' Sarah said, giving them a rueful smile. 'But we can do it on the Internet. We can find out about Henry by Googling him!'

They all grinned delightedly. Of course – there had to be something about the Graingers online.

'Tell you what,' Hannah said, 'I'll ask Miss Flood if we can use a computer at lunchtime. She'll let us if it's for the museum.'

'But what if she asks what exactly we're doing?' Abi said. 'How do we explain about Henry and all the stuff we know?'

They looked at each other – Abi was right. Miss Flood could become suspicious if they started to spout information about the Graingers.

Grace clicked her fingers. 'I've got it,' she said. 'I've been curious about the mausoleum burials – remember Simone told us it was always said to be twelve burials? Why don't we say we're trying to find out who exactly is buried down there?'

'Perfect,' said Abi, smiling at her.

Above them, the bell suddenly began to ring for the start of classes. They grabbed their bags and raced down the corridor to their classrooms.

Later, when Hannah asked Miss Flood if they could use a computer, she was delighted the girls were interested enough to want to work on the museum project by themselves. They met her at the computer room at lunch break, and she unlocked the door and told them they could have thirty minutes. Once she left, Abi and her friends crowded round a terminal and Hannah logged on. She typed 'Henry Grainger' into the search toolbar and, after a second, a list of websites popped up. They read down through them. Hannah pointed out one. 'The census records,' she said. 'That'll have something. My dad found out stuff about my great-grandfather on there.'

'And what is it?' Abi asked.

'It's like a big list of every person in the country on a particular day. Everyone had to fill out a form telling about the number of people in the family and their ages.'

They followed the link to the Census Archives website, which brought them to the census returns of 1901.

'Here goes,' said Hannah and she clicked on *Grainger, Henry* in the listing. A new page opened, with information listed under the headings: *Surname*; *Name*; *Age*; *Sex*; *Relation to Head of Family*. There were two entries under Henry's name. The girls read the page and fell silent.

'Oh no!' Abi's heart sank.

'Seriously? There is no way *I* am telling her *that*,' said Sarah. 'No way.'

They looked at each other in shock. It seemed Sarah had been right after all – the bride-to-be didn't really know Henry. There was the proof, in his own handwriting:

Surname, Name	Age	Sex	Relation to Head of Family
Grainger, Henry	33	Male	Head of Family
Grainger, Emilia	31	Female	Wife

'He left her standing at the altar after she walked eight miles and spent night after night sewing her dress and then he went and married someone else,' Grace said. 'I don't believe it!'

Hannah groaned, putting her head on the table. 'How do we tell her this?'

'Isn't it funny, though,' said Abi, thinking about it carefully, 'that they didn't have any children by then? If he left Louise-Anne to marry this Emilia, they must have been married quite a few years by 1901. That seems strange for the time, don't you think? Wouldn't it have been normal to have children quickly and lots of them?'

Sarah shrugged. 'I don't know. I've never even been kissed, so I know nothing about marriage.'

The others burst out laughing. 'Blunt as ever, Sarah,' said Hannah, shaking her head. She pressed PRINT on the screen and the printer lit up and began to churn out the page. She scrolled down through the rest of the websites referring to Henry Grainger, with Abi and the girls reading over her shoulder, but there didn't seem to be anything more about their particular Henry.

Abi still felt worried about passing on the information they'd found to Louise-Anne. She couldn't imagine how awful she would feel. 'Do you think it will help her to know this?' she asked the other girls doubtfully.

'Maybe,' said Grace. 'I suppose when she finds out he cheated she'll hate him, so that should mean she's not sad any more, right?'

Abi glanced at her watch. 'We've time for another search,' she said quickly. 'Google Emilia Grainger, just to see.'

'Good idea,' said Hannah, and she typed in the name. Again, a list of links appeared, but only one seemed to fit the bill. Hannah clicked on it and a genealogy website popped open, showing the page for Emilia Grainger.

'Her surname before she married was Dillings,' Hannah read out. 'Died in 1946. Buried in Templeton, no children, as we knew. Her father was Major William Dillings and her mother was Helen Dillings. No siblings. That's seems to be all,' she said, sounding disappointed.

'Where's Templeton?' asked Abi.

'It's a town about forty miles away from here, a small place,' Sarah replied.

'That must have been very far in those days,' Abi said. 'I wonder how they met?'

They heard a click of heels and Miss Flood popped her head round the door. 'Time to go back to class, girls,' she said. 'I need to lock up here. Did you find anything useful?'

'Yes, Miss, thanks,' Hannah said and they left quickly before she could ask any more questions. They headed down the corridor and just as they turned the corner they saw Chrissy and Elaine coming towards them. And walking from the other direction was Josh.

'Great, we're caught in the perfect storm,' Sarah muttered and the other three had to fight back laughter. Chrissy caught the look that passed between them, and her eyes narrowed in annoyance. Abi felt instantly guilty, and did her best to look friendly, but it was too late – they had rattled the hornets' nest.

'Oh, look, Elaine,' Chrissy said in her treacle-sweet voice, 'it's Grace the Madonna wannabe and her Nerd Herd friends. Been swotting up in the computer room so you can suck up to Miss Flood and get all the good jobs at the weekend, have you?'

Abi felt anger rising up in her – why did Chrissy always have to pick on Grace? She was just an easy target because she was a bit different. Out of the corner of her eye, Abi could see Josh slowing down to take in what was going on, but she didn't care any more. Let him hear, let him laugh at them if he wanted to – Chrissy had a slapdown coming to her.

Before Abi could open her mouth, Sarah stepped in front of Grace and squared off against Chrissy and Elaine.

'You are ridiculous, Chrissy,' she said, 'and you're even worse, Elaine, for going along with it like you haven't got a brain of your own to think with.'

Abi watched Chrissy for a reaction. She flicked back her loose black curls and gave Elaine a meaningful look. 'Go on, say it,' she whispered.

Elaine took a deep breath and focused on Sarah. 'You know what is ridiculous, Sarah?' she asked with a nasty smirk.

Sarah sighed impatiently. 'I don't know, Elaine. You tell me.'

'What's ridiculous is having a dad who doesn't love you enough to actually live in the same house as you.'

Sarah flinched as if Elaine had hit her. 'I . . . how do you . . .' she started, but she couldn't finish as her eyes filled with tears.

Chrissy looked half shocked, half delighted at the impact of Elaine's words on Sarah. 'Elaine's mum heard all about it,' she added meanly. '*Everyone* is talking about it.'

Abi suddenly became aware of Josh standing

right beside her. He was breathing heavily and when she turned to look at him she saw his eyes flash with anger. He stepped towards Sarah and put his hand on her arm, gently moving her backwards, away from Elaine and towards her friends. Abi couldn't help staring at his hand on Sarah's arm.

When he spoke, his voice sounded like bullets hitting home. 'Go away right now,' he said quietly. Chrissy and Elaine both blushed fiercely and looked unsure of themselves all of a sudden. 'You have no right to talk about anyone's private stuff. Leave her alone.'

'With pleasure,' retorted Chrissy, trying to gain the upper hand again. 'Come on, Elaine.' The two of them marched off down the corridor.

Josh turned to look at the girls, his face full of concern for Sarah. Her shoulders had dropped and she was struggling to hold back her tears.

'I'm sorry, Sarah,' Josh whispered. Sarah nodded, but no words came out. She was completely overcome with emotion after Elaine's outburst.

'Thank you, Josh,' Abi said quietly.

He looked at her intently and she almost reached out to touch his hand, but then he put his head down and walked away quickly.

Abi looked at Hannah, Grace and Sarah. Suddenly, she felt like an outsider again. These three had been friends for years, whereas she had never even met Sarah's parents. She wanted to say that she would leave them alone to talk, but her desire to be near Sarah and help her was even stronger.

'Sarah,' Grace said gently, 'is that true, what Elaine said about your dad?'

Sarah nodded.

'But . . . when?' Grace said, looking at Hannah, who shook her head to show she didn't know about it either.

'He left in August,' Sarah said quietly. 'I just didn't feel like talking about it.'

'Left to go where?' Abi said. Her mother had an important job in the government and she worked in the city from Monday to Friday, only coming home at the weekends, so Abi knew what it was like to have only one parent around. It felt wrong and she hated it, even though she never said so to anyone.

Sarah shrugged. 'He and Mum decided to separate. We see him most weekends though.'

'I'm so sorry,' Grace said, giving her a hug. 'Why didn't you talk to us?'

Sarah shrugged again. 'I suppose I knew that once I said it out loud, it would be real.' Her eyes filled with tears and she rested her head on Grace's shoulder. Abi and Hannah crowded round, putting their arms about her and rubbing her back.

Abi's heart broke for her friend. 'You've got us,

Sarah,' she whispered. 'You've got us.' She felt Sarah's hand reaching for hers, and she held her friend's hand tightly.

12

Pursuing Henry Grainger

When Saturday came, the girls headed to the museum with a sense of dread. Abi didn't know which she dreaded more: seeing the ghost or seeing Chrissy again. They almost expected to find Louise-Anne sitting on the doorstep, waiting for them. She wasn't there, and she wasn't in the hallway either. Abi still didn't know how they were going to tell her about Henry and Emilia – and had no idea what her reaction might be when they did.

'Right, today we want to progress things a bit more,' Miss Flood announced when everyone had gathered in the hall. The girls deliberately stood on the other side of the room from Elaine and Chrissy. Abi tried to send bad vibes across the room at them, but not before giving Josh a shy smile. He nodded at her. Her bad vibes had no effect on the two girls, though, who were acting as haughty as ever. Abi looked at them and wondered how they could sleep at night after what they'd said to Sarah. They must have hearts of stone, she decided, like those horrible tree creatures. She shook her head and turned away from the two girls in disgust.

Miss Flood was full of energy for the day's work. 'Daniel and Josh have the soundtrack more or less figured out now and we have the place looking good, so today I'd like you all to pick a room and get it fully and properly set up for visitors.'

'Shall we finish the schoolroom?' Grace asked the others.

The four girls headed off up the ornate staircase to the first floor, where the schoolroom was located at the end of the corridor. It had been used for the children of the house to be taught by a governess, so it had five desks, with attached chairs, a teacher's desk and a blackboard. There were built-in cupboards at the back of the room, stuffed with inkwells and pens and old books. The girls planned to set it up to look like the students had just gone out to play and would be back soon. There was still no sign of Louise-Anne, so they got stuck in and were soon engrossed in sorting through all the stuff in the cupboards and decking out the room. Hannah found an old Latin primer and started to copy out some verbs on to the blackboard, to make it look like the 'students' were in the middle of a Latin lesson.

'I'm glad to see you again.'

All four girls jumped at her voice. They hadn't heard a sound, but there stood Louise-Anne in the centre of the room, looking at them hopefully.

'Have you anything to tell me?' she asked, her eyes flicking from one face to the next.

They glanced at each other and wordlessly nominated Abi to do the honours yet again. Abi licked her lips and swallowed.

'We did find something,' she began. She cleared her throat. Louise-Anne was staring at her, unblinking. 'Erm . . . we found the census records for 1901 and Henry was listed there.' She stopped. She could feel her palms starting to prickle with sweat. This was not the sort of news she would have wanted to give anybody – let alone a grief-stricken ghost. 'It's not good news,' she said quietly. 'On that date in 1901, Henry was . . . married.'

For a few seconds Louise-Anne didn't move and Abi began to wonder if she'd heard her. But then the girls became aware of a low moaning sound that was slowly becoming stronger and louder. Louise-Anne began to sway from side to side, her ghostly features twisting and contorting.

Sarah leant towards Grace. 'Can ghosts explode?' she whispered.

'I hope not,' Grace whispered back, staring in horror as Louise-Anne's swaying grew faster and the moaning became a shriek.

Abi backed away slowly towards her friends.

The ghost suddenly flung back her head, her face towards the ceiling, and screamed. The girls' mouths slowly dropped open as they watched her stage a complete tantrum. She flung down her posy of flowers, followed by the letter, from which she hadn't been parted for over a hundred years. She tore at her hair and dress and threw herself against the wall. She sort of disappeared into it, but the intention was clear. She fell to her knees, then on to her back, and rolled around on the floor. She writhed and shook, and all the while her mouth twisted in that terrible scream. It went on and on. At one point, Abi edged her way to the door and peeked out, but it seemed none of the other volunteers could hear what they could – the horrible wails coming from the schoolroom. She couldn't believe it, Louise-Anne was actually making enough noise to wake the dead!

'When do you think she gets to the bit where she hates him and isn't sad any more?' Sarah said out of the corner of her mouth. 'I can't take much more of this.'

'I'm actually disappointed in her,' Grace said with a frown. The others stared at her, confused. 'Well,' she went on, 'it's only over a *boy*. I think it's all a bit embarrassing for her, to be honest.'

They couldn't help it – Grace's unique take on things had them clamping their hands over their mouths, trying to hold in their laughter. Abi lost the battle against her rising giggles once again and snorted loudly. The noise broke through Louise-Anne's tantrum and she snapped to her feet. Her eyes flashed with a black anger and the girls shivered as a numbing coldness seeped through the room.

'Are you *laughing* at me?' she demanded.

The giggles died in their throats and the girls stood stock still, terrified. Louise-Anne zoned in on Abi. 'Twice now you have laughed at me. Well, I promise you, that was the last time.' She raised her arm as if to strike out at Abi, but Grace leaped forward to put herself between them.

'NO!' she shouted. Sarah and Hannah jumped over to stand next to Grace, shielding Abi. The ghost's eyes glinted black.

'Stop this,' Hannah said, with desperation in her voice. 'Louise-Anne, you can't go throwing tantrums and trying to attack people just because you're sad. Why aren't you getting angry at Henry?'

'Yeah,' said Sarah, backing her up, 'this is the twenty-*first* century. We don't get mad any more – we get even.'

Abi breathed a sigh of relief and said a silent thank you for her brave friends.

Louise-Anne's arm slowly fell to her side. 'What do you mean?' she demanded.

'Something happened while you were dead,' Hannah said. 'It's called feminism. It means women are equal to men.'

Louise-Anne looked astonished. 'Equal?' she said, 'I never heard such a thing.' The worst of the tantrum over, Louise-Anne started to look interested. 'Tell me, what does a girl do now when a boy behaves as *he* did?'

They took it that *he* was Henry, and that *he* didn't deserve a name any more. The girls looked at each other. They were only twelve; they weren't quite sure exactly what would happen in these situations.

'Well,' said Grace uncertainly, 'a woman might go round to his place and tell the other woman that she shouldn't bother with him.' She looked at the girls for confirmation and they nodded encouragingly. That sounded possible.

'That's what I shall do!' Louise-Anne announced. 'I shall go to this *wife* and tell her that he is a dishonourable man.'

'She's long dead,' said Sarah.

'How can you be sure?' the ghost demanded. 'She might be still alive.'

'Yeah, right. Clutching at straws,' Sarah said under her breath.

Abi was terrified of the ghost's reaction if she thought she was being mocked again so she stepped in quickly. 'No, she is dead,' Abi insisted, 'we checked. Her name was Emilia and she's buried in Templeton.' She gasped and slapped her hand to her mouth. 'You're not going to go to her *grave*, are you?'

'If there's going to be a ghost catfight,' Sarah said with a wide grin, 'I am bringing the popcorn. Front-row seats.'

Louise-Anne ignored Sarah and zoned in on Abi again. 'Why is she buried there?'

'That's where they lived,' Abi replied. 'It's where they were living in 1901 anyway. And as she's buried there, it must have been her home town.'

Louise-Anne looked puzzled. 'I do not recall Henry ever going there – it was a long way distant. However did he end up marrying a girl from – *Wait!*' Suddenly, she began laughing.

'Great,' Sarah whispered to the others, 'more hysterics.'

When she finally composed herself, Louise-Anne looked at them happily. 'You have made a mistake,' she said. 'You are talking about *Charles* Grainger, Henry's brother. He had an aunt he doted on and she lived in Templeton and he went to stay with her every year. Henry never went with him. It could only be Charles who married a girl in that town.'

The girls looked at her doubtfully. 'It was written in his own handwriting,' Abi said. She wished it wasn't true, for Louise-Anne's sake. 'And it definitely said Henry – we all read it.'

'I printed it out,' Hannah said and she ran over to where she'd dropped her bag and fished out the printout of the page from the census. She brought it over and held it up in front of Louise-Anne. Again, the ghost smiled widely.

'This only serves to prove what I am saying,' she

said triumphantly. 'That is not Henry Grainger's handwriting!'

'Seriously?' said Sarah. 'How can you be sure after so long?'

Louise-Anne glided over to where her letter lay crumpled on the floor. She smoothed it out and held it up for the girls to see. She was right – the writing was completely different. 'See, I told you Henry loved me. I knew he did.'

'Oh yeah,' said Sarah, 'it looked like that's what you believed when you were screaming and writhing about on the floor.'

Louise-Anne's eyes narrowed. 'I was upset because your announcement shocked me. I never doubted him.' She glared at them. Abi decided she definitely wasn't going to say otherwise.

'It still doesn't make sense though,' Hannah said. 'Who signed the census? If it was Charles, why did he use Henry's name? There must be more to this. We still don't know why Henry didn't get to the church.'

'How are you going to find out?' Louise-Anne demanded.

They all looked at Hannah. She shrugged. 'More research, I suppose,' she said. 'I'll check the library here. And, Grace –' she turned to look at her – 'why don't you ask permission to go to the parish records place? It'll be open now. We have to be able to find out something more there.'

But Abi could see that Louise-Anne was lost in her memories again, staring out of the window.

'Henry,' the ghost bride whispered.

13

Records and Rumours

The girls raced down the stairs to find Miss Flood standing in the hallway, talking to Simone.

'Hey, Simone,' Grace said, smiling at her. 'Checking up on us?'

'Just curious to see how you've been getting on.' Simone smiled back. 'The house is looking really great.'

'Miss Flood,' Grace said, 'may I cycle to the library? I want to check something in the parish records – it's to do with the Graingers. I want to check the burial records.'

Miss Flood looked hesitant, so Hannah said quickly, 'We're still curious about the burials in the mausoleum. We'd like to draw up an accurate list of the burials, if we can. We need to be able to give visitors that information, don't you think?'

Miss Flood nodded. 'Yes, you're right. I don't want to repeat an incorrect fact. OK, Grace. You can go, but take one other person with you and stay together. I'll ring Miss Belsham at the records office right now,' she said, pulling her mobile out of her pocket, 'to tell her you're coming and will be there in twenty minutes. So no dawdling,' she warned. 'Go straight there, all right?'

'Yes, Miss,' Grace promised. She turned to Sarah. 'You've got your bike today, haven't you?' Sarah nodded. 'Will you come with me?' The two girls headed off.

'May I look at some of the books in the library?' Hannah asked Miss Flood. 'I thought I might find something there too. Abi, come with me?'

Abi nodded, glad of something to do that might help Louise-Anne.

'I can help you both with that as well,' Simone said, 'if that's OK with you.' She turned to Miss Flood. 'I know a lot of the books in there, so I might be able to find what you need.'

Simone, Abi and Hannah went into the small library together. It had floor-to-ceiling shelves, all filled with books. It was Hannah's idea of heaven. Abi bet that when she was older Hannah would build a room just like this in her own house.

'OK, what do you want to look at?' Simone asked them both.

'I'd like to read about the Graingers around 1900,' Hannah said, 'and about the burials in the mausoleum.'

'Well, there's a biography that some guy wrote about us and that's got stuff about all of the family members up to 1950. I suppose that would be a good start?'

'Great,' Hannah said as Simone looked along one of the shelves for the book.

'You're really interested in the mausoleum, aren't you?' Simone said, as she combed through the shelf.

'Yeah,' said Abi. 'Ever since we realized there's an extra burial down there, we've wanted to find out about it and solve the mystery.'

'I hope this helps,' Simone said, pulling a hardback book off the shelf and bringing it over to the reading table. Heads bent together, the three girls flicked through the pages. 'Here,' Simone said, pointing to a black-and-white photo of the mausoleum. The caption underneath said there were twelve burials in the mausoleum. 'There it is,' Simone said, straightening up, 'they got it wrong.'

Miss Belsham smiled at Grace and Sarah. 'Now, girls, what can I help you with exactly?'

'We'd like to look up some information on Henry Grainger, please,' Grace said.

'Is this your first time here?' Miss Belsham asked.

'Yes, thank you, we have lives,' Sarah said with a cheeky grin.

Miss Belsham peered at Sarah over the top of her glasses. 'Well, well, well,' she said brightly, 'someone call the king and tell him I've found his jester.' Grace and Sarah made a face behind her back as Miss Belsham turned on her heel and clicked off into one of the aisles. The room had six aisles, each one leading between shelves stacked tight with papers and old logbooks. 'We have an awful lot on the various Graingers,' she called out. 'Can you be any more specific?'

Grace and Sarah looked at each other. 'Er, well, maybe information on Henry's wife and where they lived and died,' Grace said. Sarah nodded in agreement.

'Just give me a moment,' came the reply. 'Sit down at the desk there and I'll bring over the relevant papers.'

They pulled out chairs and sat at the round oak table that was next to Miss Belsham's desk, which stood on a dais. They heard the *click-click* of her heels returning and she laid a folder on the table in front of them. It had HENRY GRAINGER printed on the front in neat capitals.

'Wow!' said Grace. 'I didn't think it would be that easy.'

Miss Belsham smiled at her. 'I run a very tight ship here. Now, will that do for the time being?'

'Yes, thanks,' Grace said. The two girls started going through the folder. Henry was born in 1868, to Celia and Joshua Grainger. It listed his siblings and their birth dates. Grace flicked ahead, looking for the death records. 'Here it is,' she said excitedly.

They read the information: *Henry Grainger d. 1916, Templeton, and received the Last Rites at home; interred in the Grainger family mausoleum, at the house where he was born.*

Grace looked at Sarah. 'Do you think he died while visiting Charles and Emilia?'

'Bit of a coincidence,' Sarah replied. 'Let's look for marriage certificates.'

'There's none in here. Hang on,' Grace said. 'Excuse me, Miss Belsham,' she said loudly. 'May we check for Henry's marriage certificate – it doesn't seem to be here?'

'No, they're stored separately,' Miss Belsham replied. 'It's on microfiche. Let me get the right sheet.' She went to a large filing cabinet and extracted another folder, which she brought over to the desktop reader in the corner. 'Come here, girls, and I'll show you how to use this machine.' She placed the microfiche sheet on the reader and switched it on, then turned a wheel on the side to scroll through the records stored on the microfiche.

'I've never seen one of those before,' Sarah remarked. 'It's really good.'

'So there are still some things you don't know, are there, madam?' Miss Belsham said, smiling to herself. She continued flicking through the images, then came to a halt. 'Here we are,' she said.

The girls craned forward eagerly and Grace read

aloud: '*Henry Grainger and Emilia Dillings were united in holy matrimony on this day, fourth of November, in the year of our Lord 1886* . . .' Her mouth fell open. 'Sarah, he *did* marry Emilia and just *four days* after dumping Louise-Anne!'

'Who's Louise-Anne?' Miss Belsham asked immediately. 'How do you know about Henry Grainger's love life, may I ask?'

Grace and Sarah flushed guiltily. 'We . . . um . . .' stuttered Grace.

'We're just working on something, but we're not sure of the facts yet,' Sarah said quickly.

'Well, tell me more,' said Miss Belsham impatiently. 'I can help solve it, whatever it is.'

Grace looked at her watch. 'I'm sorry, but we really need to get back,' she said. 'I promise we'll fill you in when we've figured it out.'

Miss Belsham pursed her lips and looked from the marriage certificate to the girls. 'But what could be odd about it?' she asked.

'Henry was buried in the Grainger mausoleum,' Sarah said. 'Emilia was buried in Templeton. Why would that be?'

Miss Belsham frowned. 'She wasn't buried with him? Well, it's a bit odd, I grant you, but hardly unheard of – they could have agreed to be buried in family plots. Are you absolutely sure she was buried elsewhere?'

The girls nodded. 'We saw it online,' Sarah

replied. 'Was Henry definitely buried in the mausoleum?'

'Yes.' Miss Belsham nodded. 'It's in every record I've ever seen about the burials there. But look, you can't take what you read online as gospel. There's a good chance what you read is wrong and Emilia *is* in the Grainger mausoleum. Maybe she's under her maiden name, or even had a different first name – sometimes people were christened with one name, but ended up being called by a pet name. I really wouldn't hold with what the Internet says – you need to read it in an actual book, girls.'

'OK, well then, would you have a list of the family members in the mausoleum and their death dates?' Grace asked. 'We would like to include it in the information for visitors when the museum opens.'

'Yes, I have that,' Miss Belsham said. 'I can photocopy it for you.' She bustled off again and emerged from a different aisle with yet another folder. She took out the relevant piece of paper and crossed over to the small photocopier and made a copy for them. As she handed it to Grace she said, 'Emilia isn't listed there, but, as I said, there could be a good reason for that. I'll contact the Templeton parish records office and double-check on her. I should have the information on Monday and I'll call Miss Flood and tell her what I find out. And if you need anything else for the museum just say the word.'

'Thank you so much,' the girls said, smiling. 'We'd really better get off now. We'll be in touch. Bye.'

Miss Belsham watched them leave, then went to the phone and made two phone calls: one to Olivia Flood, to tell her the girls were on the way back; and one to Mr Davenport, who ran the local history office in Templeton. This little nugget of information from the two girls had sparked her interest.

When Grace and Sarah got back to the house, they went straight to the library, where Abi and Hannah were waiting excitedly for them. Simone had gone to talk to Miss Flood.

'What did you find out?' Hannah demanded.

'He married her,' Sarah announced. 'And you will *not* believe this – he married her on the fourth of November! We saw the marriage certificate.'

'Jeez,' said Abi, thinking how the news just got worse and worse for poor Louise-Anne. 'A two-timer!'

'Keep your voices down,' hissed Hannah. 'We don't want her hearing and having another freak attack.'

'The other thing,' Grace whispered, 'is that he *is* buried here, in the mausoleum. Miss Belsham said that's definite. Look, here's a list of all the bodies in there, and he's on it.' They looked at the list, which had each of the names of those interred in the mausoleum, with a death date beside each one and in brackets afterwards either *cremation* or *burial*. Henry was there: *1916 (burial)*.

'Did you two find out anything else?' Grace asked.

'Maybe,' said Hannah. 'We also read that he was married to Emilia and lived in Templeton – it definitely wasn't Charles – but there's something else. There's a rumour about a duel that was said to have taken place between the Grainger brothers and a man from another parish, that's what it says. The guy writing the book says –' Hannah looked down and began reading it word for word – '*it was never substantiated, but rumours persisted that on the night of thirty-first October 1886 some sort of altercation took place at which both Henry and Charles Grainger were present. One elderly resident of the town told me that it was a duel fought for the love of a beautiful woman, but that seems a little fanciful. After all, the last duel was fought in this country around 1865.*'

Abi looked at her friends. 'On the night of thirty-first October,' she whispered. 'That's the night he was meant to marry Louise-Anne.' Before she could say another word, there was a breath of cold air and the hairs stood up on her arms. The air shimmered in the corner of the library and the ghost of Louise-Anne appeared before them.

'It is true, then?' Louise-Anne said in a mournful voice. 'He did marry this woman?'

'Yes, he did,' Hannah said gently. 'But, Louise-Anne, there might still be more to this story. There could have been a duel on your wedding night. We have to find out about that before we can say for sure what happened with Henry.'

Louise-Anne's lips parted, but no sound came out. Her face looked so sad that Abi felt tears spring up in her eyes. She looked over at her friends, and their eyes were shining with tears too. The ghost's whole being seemed to sag under the weight of this evidence, as if she were being physically crushed by sorrow. It was awful to see, but impossible to look away. The air began to shimmer around her again and she disappeared without another word. As the girls stood there tearfully, staring at the spot where she had been, the door swung open and Simone walked in. She stared at the girls in confusion.

'What's happened?' she asked, her voice full of concern. 'Are you OK?'

The girls pulled themselves together and attempted to smile at her. 'No, no, we're fine,' Hannah said. Simone didn't look convinced – at all.

'I won't ask,' she said quietly, 'but if I can help you with anything do let me know. Now,' she said briskly, 'you are wanted over in the sitting room with the other volunteers.'

She walked out and the girls looked at each other.

'She knows something's up,' Grace whispered.

'I know, but what can we do?' Abi said, biting her lip.

As they headed outside Sarah said gloomily, 'I hope you're right and there's more to Henry's story, otherwise his jilted bride is going to have a very long and sad eternity.'

All of the volunteers were in the sitting room with Miss Flood and Simone.

'Sit down, girls,' Miss Flood said. 'You can fill me in on your research later, but for now I want to talk about something very exciting. A grand opening!'

'We're going to have a grand opening?' Jack said, surprised. 'I didn't know that was part of the plan.'

'It wasn't,' Miss Flood said. 'But you've all worked so hard and done such a good job – better than I expected, to be honest – that I think we should celebrate the opening properly. Now, today is the eighteenth of October,' she said, 'and I've had what I'll hope you agree is a very good idea. How about we host an opening night on Friday the thirty-first – Hallowe'en! We can theme the party, have pumpkins and that sort of thing, and send a general invitation to the town. What do you think – can we do it?'

They all started talking at once and Miss Flood held up her hands for silence. 'Hang on, hang on,' she said with a laugh. 'First things first – do you think we can pull it off in just two more weeks?'

The children looked around at each other. 'We can be ready,' Daniel said, nodding over at Josh.

'Yes, it shouldn't be a problem,' Solomon said. 'We've made a start on every room.'

'Perhaps we should start getting paid overtime?' Chrissy said, with an edge in her voice. Miss Flood chose to ignore that remark.

'Well, that's settled then,' their teacher said, looking pleased. 'We'll aim to have a launch party on Hallowe'en night, then we'll open to the public for the first time the following day.'

Abi almost clapped her hands in excitement.

Grace put up her hand. 'I've a suggestion, Miss,' she said, 'but it will cost a little bit of money.'

Miss Flood frowned. 'There really isn't much in the budget, Grace, so it has to be absolutely essential.'

'Well,' Grace continued, 'I was just thinking it would be a good idea for us to have some kind of uniform, so visitors can find us easily. I'd like to make T-shirts for us to wear.'

'Oh,' said Miss Flood. 'I hadn't thought about that. How much would it cost?'

'Not much at all,' Grace replied. 'I've already approached Morton's in the town, and they said they'd let me have eleven T-shirts for just twenty pounds, that's half price. And the printing I have in mind would add another twenty – although I might get that reduced too once I explain what it's for.'

Abi looked at her friend admiringly – she was so full of get up and go.

'Well, we can find that much,' said Miss Flood, smiling. 'Go ahead with it, Grace.'

'I'm sorry,' said Chrissy, 'does anyone else have a problem with that?'

Abi felt her whole body tense up. It was the first time Chrissy had dared speak to them since the incident in the corridor. Remembering that made her look over at Josh. He was watching Chrissy with a wary expression. Abi thought he looked ready to step in again, if he needed to. 'Just look at how she dresses,' Chrissy said, gesturing at Grace, who was wearing a tight green cardigan decorated with tiny red kittens, a yellow shirt under that which she'd let stick out over her peach-coloured pleated skirt, and a pair of brown ankle boots. 'There's no way I want *her* styling me. We'll all end up looking like weirdos – like she does.'

'I second that,' Elaine said.

'It'll be just a T-shirt,' Grace said quietly. 'Nothing unusual.'

'Yeah, right,' Chrissy snapped. 'It'll probably have crazy puff sleeves or some weird shape.'

'Nope,' said Grace, 'they're just plain old T-shirts from Morton's, that's all.'

'Well, I'm having a final say in whether I wear it or not, once I've seen it.'

But today Josh didn't need to stick up for the girls. Miss Flood spoke up instead. 'You, Chrissy Edwards and Elaine Pearson, will wear what you're given. And that's final.'

This time, Abi didn't even bother to try to hold in her laughter. *Let Chrissy know how ridiculous she sounds*, she thought to herself. *It's better than letting her think she's actually making sense.*

14

Back to the Gate Lodge

The following day was Sunday and Abi found it impossible to think about anything other than the ghost and her missing groom. It seemed she wasn't the only one: her mobile beeped and a message came through from Sarah that had obviously been sent to the other girls too.

> Anyone free to meet up?
> Can't get Louise-Anne out of my head.
> I think we should try something else.

By the time Abi arrived at Sarah's, Hannah and Grace were already there and busy making sandwiches for the four of them.

'So I've been thinking,' Sarah said when they were sitting down at the table, 'why don't we try to find out if Emilia is buried here ourselves, rather than waiting for Miss Belsham to find out?'

'But what would it tell us about Henry?' Abi asked.

'I'm not sure,' Sarah said with a frown, 'but, if she's not buried here, could it mean they weren't very happily married? I mean, Abi, you pointed out that they didn't have kids, which was unusual at that time. And normally married people are buried together, aren't they? So, if they weren't, it would probably mean something that might be a clue for us.'

'Okaaay,' said Abi, not sounding very sure, 'and how do we find that out?'

'Simone,' Sarah replied. 'I've been thinking about it. As the town undertakers, the Graingers must hold records of all burials – especially anyone who qualifies as a relative. I bet there's a record in the gate lodge.'

The girls looked at each other. 'It's worth a shot,' Hannah said.

Sarah told her mum they were going to the gate lodge and that it had to do with the museum project. 'Just text your parents and tell them,' she said to the other girls, and then the four of them headed off on their bikes.

When they reached the gate lodge, Abi knocked softly at the door, hoping there wasn't a 'client' arriving today. They didn't want to get in the way. Simone opened the door. She looked happy to see them.

'Come on in,' she said with a smile. 'What can I do for you today?'

She led them back to the sitting room they had sat in last time. It was a cosy room with two fat armchairs, a sofa and walls lined with bookshelves. The fire was burning in the grate, just as before. Abi looked about at the interesting objects around the room, trying to read the spines of the books, as Hannah told Simone what they had discovered so far about Henry, leaving out the sighting of Louise-Anne. That seemed like it would be a story too far for Simone to take in.

'And so you see,' Hannah concluded, 'we're thinking now that there was something odd about Henry's marriage, but we don't know what. Would you be able to check if Emilia was buried in this town?'

'I have the records for the main town graveyard,' Simone said. 'There are two smaller ones, though you'd have to go back to Miss Belsham about those. But, certainly, we know who's in the big cemetery.' She looked at them, her head cocked to one side. 'Are you absolutely sure she's not in our mausoleum though?'

'Well, you'd know if she was, right?' said Abi.

Simone frowned. 'I've heard of Henry all right, but Emilia I don't know. I suppose if she was in our place I'd have heard of her, but it just seems odd.' She frowned again. 'Tell you what,' she said, 'I'll check our records for you for the town cemetery, but we may as well make the most of all the expertise we have here, which means my dad. I'll ask him about Henry, see if he knows anything about it.'

'Thanks, Simone,' Abi and Hannah said at the same time, then they broke into giggles.

Simone led them down the hallway and into a low-ceilinged room on the right: the records room. 'So when do you think Emilia died?' she asked.

'About 1946,' Hannah replied, settling herself into a hard-backed chair at the small round table in the centre of the room.

Simone went to the relevant section and began searching through the files. Eventually, she picked out a large record book and brought it over to the table where the girls were sitting. She opened it up and thumbed gently through the pages.

'G, G, G . . .' she muttered as she searched. 'Here we go.' She ran her finger down the list of entries. 'Nope,' she said, looking up at them. 'Emilia Grainger née Dillings is not here. Not in the main cemetery at any rate.'

'Could we check another one?' Abi said suddenly. 'Louise-Anne Miller.'

The other girls started at the mention of her name. Simone's eyes narrowed, but didn't ask who she was. 'Sure,' she said, returning the book to the shelves. 'What year did she die?'

'1886,' said Abi.

'OK,' said Simone, scanning along the relevant shelf. 'Should be here.'

Simone pulled out a dusty book, blew the cover gently and brought it over to them. She turned to the Ms and ran her finger down the page. She stopped near the bottom 'Miller, Louise-Anne,' she said. 'Here she is. In the town cemetery, section H, row four.'

'Thank you,' Abi said, looking at her. 'It's just someone I read about and I'd like to . . . lay some flowers . . . or something.' Her voice trailed off and she blushed.

'Hmmm,' Simone said thoughtfully. 'That's interesting. It looks like she has something in our vault. There's an asterisk by her name.'

'In the vault?' Hannah said sharply. 'Here? In the gate lodge?'

'Yeah,' Simone said, nodding. 'I told you about the deposit boxes. An asterisk means someone deposited something in a box in her name.' She looked down at the book again. 'In fact, unless that's a mistake, it actually looks like she has two boxes, which is unusual.'

The girls glanced at each other. Who could have done that? What could be in them?

'Who is allowed to open the boxes?' Hannah asked. 'Does it say?'

'No,' said Simone, shaking her head. 'It just indicates that there are boxes, so there must be something in them, I guess.'

Abi felt excitement rising in her chest. Surely

there had to be, at the very least, a clue in the boxes? She was trying to think how to ask Simone to let them look in the deposit boxes when the door swung open and Mr Grainger walked in.

'Lovely to see you all again,' he smiled. 'Funny way to spend a visit, though,' he said, looking around the room. 'Aren't girls supposed to huddle together and giggle about boys?' he teased.

'Dad!' Simone said, blushing. 'Don't be so silly. I was just helping the girls with some of the Grainger history.'

'Oh, really?' he said with great interest. 'And who has caught your attention?'

'It was Henry to begin with,' Simone said, 'but now they've asked about a Louise-Anne Miller?'

Mr Grainger frowned. 'That rings a bell . . . but I'm having a senior moment – can't recall exactly . . . Who was she?'

Simone swung round to face the girls. 'Yes,' she said, her eyebrow raised, '*who* was she?'

The girls looked at each other – how could they tell the truth? But wouldn't the Graingers know if they were lying? Abi decided to be honest, but give very little detail. 'As far as we can tell, she was a local girl who had some sort of a . . . relationship with Henry Grainger. We've been reading books in the library at the house and have also been down with Miss Belsham, trying to figure out why Henry married Emilia and not Louise-Anne.' She took a deep breath – no lies in all that.

'And,' Simone said, 'it would appear that this Louise-Anne Miller has two deposit boxes in the vault.'

'Ah, *that's* why the name is familiar,' Mr Grainger said, nodding. 'I knew I'd heard it before. She's the only person to have two boxes. Of course, that's why it rang a bell. Explain to me again why all this is relevant.'

Oh no, thought Abi, *how do I manage this without telling blatant lies?* Luckily, Grace had seen Abi's panicked expression and stepped in. 'All we know,' Grace said carefully, 'is that Henry perhaps promised to marry Louise-Anne. There is a story that they arranged to meet to marry secretly, but he never turned up. Then we found an account of a rumour that, on the same night he was meant to marry, there was some sort of duel involving him and his brother. Whatever happened, four days later he married Emilia.'

'That's intriguing all right,' said Mr Grainger thoughtfully. 'I always presumed that Emilia wished to be buried with her parents and Henry with his. I didn't think it was strange.'

'It might not be,' Hannah agreed, 'but it would be good to know if it was in any way linked to this other woman, Miller.'

'You know, I do recall that name now,' Mr

Grainger said. 'I remember my father mentioning that the Miller family had two boxes. Then years later there was a fellow came here once; he was doing a local archaeological project and wanted to do a geophysical survey of the cemetery, which involved using physical sensing techniques to create a map of what's hidden beneath the surface – fascinating stuff. He was a poet into the bargain and afterwards he wrote a poem about it and it had a funny line about *taking soundings and one grave remains silent.* I met him one day in the town and I asked him about it. He said he had completed the project, but couldn't explain why one grave didn't return a result – he said it was like there was nothing in it. And that was the name on the grave: Louise-Anne Miller. I'd forgotten that until now,' he said. He looked at the girls again. 'So you have some reason to think there's a link between Henry and Louise-Anne? Hmmm. Let me go and check something and I'll come back to you.'

When he was gone, Simone stared intently at the girls. 'So are you going to tell *me* the truth?' she said in a quiet voice. 'I know something was happening in the house yesterday.'

The girls looked at each other. Could they trust Simone? Hannah nodded slowly and Grace and Sarah smiled their agreement.

'Do you want to know the truth?' Abi replied, looking her in the eye.

Simone considered this for a moment and then said, 'Yes, I do. I think I can guess what it is, but I'd like to hear it.'

Abi glanced towards the door, but there was no sound of Mr Grainger returning. She leant towards Simone and whispered, 'After we left you, when we returned the diary, we all did the ritual that night.'

'Exactly like Beryl said,' Grace added.

'We thought it was a bit of fun,' Abi continued, 'but a week later we met her. Louise-Anne Miller.'

She looked at Simone, expecting her to laugh and call them idiots, but Simone was listening closely. 'Go on,' she prompted.

'She was wearing a white dress – her wedding dress, it turned out – and she was so sad. She told us that she loved Henry and he loved her, and her dad was trying to get her to marry some other guy when she turned sixteen, but she wanted Henry. So he asked her to marry him, she said yes and they arranged to marry in secret, but he never turned up. He left her standing at the altar. He sent her a letter, saying he couldn't marry her, but she never believed it. She died two days later from fever, and she's haunted by her loss and asked us to find out why he never came to her.'

Simone looked from one girl to the next. 'And you all saw her?' she asked. Four heads nodded in agreement. She sat back. 'That's incredible,' she said.

'Do you believe us?' Grace said.

'I believe you,' said Simone. 'I've never seen anything, like I said, but I read Beryl's diary again and . . . well, who am I to say what is and isn't possible?' She blew her fringe out of her eyes. 'And this girl, Louise-Anne, she was only my age when all this happened?'

'Yes,' they said, nodding.

'Wow,' Simone said, shaking her head. 'That is heavy stuff.'

Grace leant closer and whispered, 'Would you like to do the ritual too, Simone? Then you could help us – we'd be ghost detectives together.'

Simone smiled at her. 'Thanks for thinking of me, Grace,' she said, 'but no, it's not for me. Beryl talked about it as a mixed blessing, and I can see how that might be the case. But I'm always here to help, whenever you need it.'

They could hear the *swish-swish* of Mr Grainger's slippers coming back down the hallway. 'We really want to help her,' Abi said quickly. 'She is so heartbroken. She can't rest until she knows why he betrayed her.'

The door opened again and Mr Grainger came back in, carrying a mottled logbook in his hands. His eyes were bright. 'Well, well, well,' he said, smiling, 'I think things just got a little more interesting. This is the original entry book from the vault, where each deposit is recorded in greater detail. I'm not going to show it to you because that would break our rules, but I can tell you about the Miller boxes because they are no longer under the guarantee of privacy.'

All five girls were hanging on his every word. What would the boxes tell them?

'The first box,' Mr Grainger began, 'was rented and paid for by Mr Aloysius Miller, who stated his relation to the deceased as "father". He placed three items on deposit, although it doesn't say what they are. He paid a sum to cover the rental for a period of ninety-nine years, which time has elapsed.'

'What does that mean?' Hannah asked breathlessly.

'It means it is now the property of Grainger Undertakers, and that we may look inside,' Mr Grainger said slowly, enjoying the looks on their faces.

'What is even more interesting,' he said, 'is the identity of the person who rented the second deposit box.' He paused for effect.

'Who, who?' Sarah practically shouted.

Mr Grainger smiled. 'It was none other than my ancestor, Henry Grainger.'

'So there *is* a link,' Simone said, looking at the girls.

'He left her something,' Hannah said, her eyes shining. 'Surely that means he did love her?'

Abi felt like doing a jig on the spot – this was so much more than they'd hoped for. 'May we look in Henry's deposit box?' she asked Mr Grainger, crossing her fingers tightly as she waited for his reply.

'Perhaps,' he said. 'There are rules about the boxes and accessing them, but, as Henry is a family member, I am permitted to open the box. However –' he held up a hand before the girls started whooping with delight – 'however, there is Grainger family protocol to be observed. There is an agreement in place that no family deposit box can be opened without the consent of all living Graingers, which means I shall have to contact each one in turn and secure agreement to proceed.'

'Well, you have my permission,' Simone said, grinning. 'I think these girls are on to a good story here and I want to hear the ending.'

'And you have my permission,' Mr Grainger said, 'but there are Graingers scattered about the world, so it's going to take a little time. I'll start making calls and emails first thing in the morning.'

'Thank you so, so much,' Abi said, her eyes sparkling. The girls hugged each other with anticipation.

'Well, now,' said Mr Grainger, 'would you like to see what's in the Miller box?'

15

Deposit Boxes

The two Graingers and the four girls made their way down the corridor, then through a short glass tunnel that connected the old gate lodge to the modern extension. They walked past a door with MORGUE written on it and made their way to the other end of the building. There was a door with a sign in red lettering: STRICTLY PRIVATE — NO ADMITTANCE TO UNAUTHORIZED PERSONNEL. Mr Grainger opened that door, then locked it again behind them. It all felt very secret and mysterious and Abi felt a tingle of excitement building inside her. By the looks on the other girls' faces, she could tell her friends felt the same.

They stood in a very small space, facing a second door, which was made of steel and looked like it would be impossible to break into. Mr Grainger used a large key to clank it open and ushered them through, before once again locking it behind them. They were now standing at the top of a spiral staircase that led down below, into the basement.

'This is seriously good!' Sarah said, her eyes wide in amazement.

'It's like Fort Knox,' Abi said.

'This way,' Mr Grainger said, leading them down the steep staircase.

The stairs curled down into the bottom level, where they found themselves in a barrel-vaulted room. They were standing in a little connecting corridor and on their left was a wide, semi-circular alcove that was ringed with floor-to-ceiling deposit boxes, while on their right was a smaller semi-circular alcove in which was placed a long table with eight chairs around it.

'If you could take a seat at the table,' Mr Grainger said, motioning towards the other alcove as he pulled on a pair of white gloves, 'I'll go and fetch the Miller box.'

They went into the alcove and sat down, straining to see what he was doing. Grace looked around in wonder. 'What's kept in the boxes, Simone, that it has to be protected like this?' she said.

'As a rule,' Simone replied, 'we don't know. It's best that only the box owner knows what's in there.'

Mr Grainger came towards them carrying a long, heavy-looking box with a brass handle at the front. He placed it carefully on the table, then unlocked it with an odd-shaped little key and slid off the lid. Six heads pressed close as they all bent to see the contents of the box. Mr Grainger removed each one with great care: a book of Shakespeare's sonnets, an unusual gold ring made of two bands joined together and a letter.

'It's her book,' Hannah said in delight. 'The one Henry gave her in the garden. Can we see the first page?' she asked Mr Grainger eagerly. He gently opened the book and there on the title page was the inscription:

For Miss Louise-Anne Miller. From H.G.

'Oh wow,' said Abi, feeling like she might start crying – or laughing, knowing her. 'May we read the letter?' she asked in a whisper.

Mr Grainger gently removed the paper from the box and unfolded it. Then he began to read:

My darling Louise-Anne,
Tonight I sit by the light of a candle, unable to rest because I am without you. My darling child, I have lost you. Last night, the doctor was called in the early hours, but, by the time he reached us, you were gone. My only girl, I must live with the sorrow that this is my doing. I wanted you to break with the Grainger boy for good because I only wanted what was right for you. I cannot confess my crime to anyone, so I will confess it here. When you began spending time at the Grainger house, I took into my employment a woman who worked there, begging her to give me any information

about you and the Graingers. It was from her that I learned of the plan to marry – she had spied on Henry and his brother from one of the hidden corridors and heard all. On that night, I let you go, my child, happy in your belief that you were to meet him. I watched the church all night, and saw you arrive. Long after daybreak, a horse and rider approached and I stopped the rider. He was a messenger, with a letter from the Grainger boy explaining that he could not come, but loved you still and would come soon to explain all. I paid the rider to hand over that letter to me, and I tore it up. Then I made him pen a new missive to you, declaring there was no love between you any more and I paid him to take it to the priest. If I had but known what that action would lead to, my darling girl. I weep as I inscribe these lines, this meagre confession. I let you walk home, thinking it would cool your passion and you would return to me as my own sweet daughter, just as you were before he stole your heart. But I was never to have that sweet girl returned to me.

This morning, as we were making the preparations for your burial, a small package arrived, addressed to you. Inside, I found the double ring: he had welded together your wedding bands. I can only think it was a sign to you that you were his true love. It arrived too late – for you and for me. My little one, forgive me. I will never forgive myself, but I need your forgiveness. A father's lot is difficult – there is a strong desire to keep a daughter close, to hold on to that irreplaceable love, but I was wrong. It no longer matters, Louise-Anne, because I can never tell you, but I was wrong. I love you, my darling daughter.

Silence greeted the end of the letter. Even Mr Grainger seemed affected by it. 'Poor man,' he muttered to himself. 'That's a dreadful thing to live with.' The girls couldn't speak for a few minutes. They were trying to digest what the letter had told them: that Henry did love Louise-Anne and had delivered the joined-together weddings rings as a sign of that love, and that it was Louise-Anne's own father who had prevented the marriage and unwittingly caused her death. It was mind-boggling.

'Thank you, Mr Grainger,' Abi said quietly, 'that clears up an awful lot.'

Mr Grainger replaced the box as carefully as he had removed it and they made their way out of the vault and back up to the gate lodge, then out into the light once more. At the door they said goodbye to Simone, who smiled warmly at them. 'Cheer up,' she said gently. 'I know it's a lot to get to grips with, but at least you can help her now – you can tell her that he did love her, that's what she wanted to know.'

'No, that's not it,' Hannah sighed. 'She asked us *why* he didn't come to the church and, without his letter that the rider was bringing, we still can't answer that.'

'Plus,' said Sarah gloomily, 'if we tell her about the rings, we will have to say where we found them, and then we'd have to tell her about the letter. I really couldn't tell her what her father did. To feel that your own father doesn't love you enough is . . .' She stopped and ran her hand through her long red hair. 'Well, I just don't want to be the one to tell her that. I don't think any of us would.'

Simone sighed and wished she could give them heart in some way. 'Dad will get the permission for the other box,' she promised. 'Then we'll find out what Henry himself wanted her to know. That has to be the final bit of the puzzle, doesn't it?'

The girls nodded tiredly and waved goodbye. Their minds were buzzing with the events of the past hour.

Grace looked at her friends as they walked towards the bikes. 'Is anyone else feeling like it would be lovely to be flicking through *Girl Talk* and gossiping about daft things right now, instead of all this?' she asked.

'Too late now,' Hannah said glumly.

16

Rest in Peace

The following Saturday morning, the volunteers were in great spirits. It helped the girls to put Louise-Anne out of their minds. They had argued about what to tell her and finally decided to hold off saying anything about the letter and the ring today. None of them felt ready for that particular conversation.

In the house, there was a feeling of urgency to their work now because they all wanted the museum to be perfect for the night of the launch party, which was only a week away. They had made good progress with the exhibits in the rooms. Each room was set up as if the family still lived there, with the more interesting items laid out on tables. They had all copied out note cards to stand beside each object, explaining its history and use. It was starting to look like a real museum at last.

'Gather round here in the hallway,' Miss Flood called out. 'Today, I want everyone to work on the reception area. It's very important because it's the first thing visitors see when they step through the front door, so it has to be welcoming. We need to scrub it clean and then set it up. OK, let's get to work!'

'Where are you going, Miss?' Jack asked as Miss Flood started to walk away.

'To get more cleaning supplies from the kitchen,' she called back over her shoulder. 'You can get started.'

Jack turned to face the others and grinned. 'Whenever she says, "Let's get to work," she always walks away and doesn't start work at all!'

Solomon laughed. 'Yeah, I've noticed that too,' he said. 'Some people definitely work harder than others around here.'

'I think Josh and I work hardest of all,' Daniel said, joining in. Josh smiled.

'Yeah, right,' they all shouted in unison, and Daniel laughed.

'It's true!' he protested.

'I've carried so many pieces of furniture up those stairs,' Sarah said. 'I think I'd get the medal for best volunteer.'

'No way!' Daniel said, giving her a cheeky poke in the arm. 'You're just a girl. Girls don't ever work as hard as boys.'

'Hey!' all the girls cried out together. Josh laughed out loud and Abi turned in surprise. He smiled at her and Abi couldn't help but smile back.

'Boys!' Grace said, shaking her head.

Sarah glanced towards the back stairs. 'I think Miss Flood's on her way back. Look busy!'

They scattered to different parts of the hallway and looked the picture of industry when Miss Flood walked in with a bucket and mop and some dustcloths. Still grinning at each other, they set to work on the reception area with gusto.

They had been working hard for almost two hours when they heard a car pull up on the gravel outside, doors slamming shut, then the sound of footsteps approaching the front door. The heavy door swung open and there stood Mr Grainger and Simone, smiling widely. As Mr Grainger stepped into the hallway, Abi, Hannah, Sarah and Grace gasped – he was carrying two deposit boxes from the vault.

'Hello again,' he said. 'I think I've got something here that's going to interest you.'

'Is that . . . Henry's box for Louise-Anne?' Hannah asked.

'Yes, it is,' said Mr Grainger. The four girls couldn't say a word – this was just too much!

'What's all this?' Miss Flood asked, very curious about what Mr Grainger was holding.

'Let's go into the drawing room and we'll explain it,' Mr Grainger said.

'Can we come too?' Daniel asked.

'Of course,' said Mr Grainger. 'The more, the merrier.'

Abi felt a pang of regret that part of their secret was about to be shared with the rest of the volunteers, but at least Louise-Anne was still theirs and theirs alone. The others hadn't seen her in the mausoleum that day and couldn't hear her when she'd wailed like a mad woman in the house, so she'd remain the girls' secret.

As they made their way in, Simone smiled excitedly at the girls. 'This is going to be good!' she whispered.

When everyone was seated, Mr Grainger said, 'Now, before we open these boxes, I'd like one of the girls to explain what has happened up to this point, so you all understand what the boxes are and their significance.'

'Is this to do with the research you were doing on the burials in the mausoleum?' Miss Flood asked the girls.

'It's to do with Henry Grainger,' Sarah said, 'and some new things we found out about him.'

'New things?' Miss Flood said, sounding surprised. 'That's fantastic – good work, girls!'

Chrissy and Elaine both scowled at Miss Flood's praise of the girls.

'So,' Mr Grainger said, 'who'd like to do the explaining?'

'I'll do it,' Abi said, jumping out of her chair and walking up to stand beside Mr Grainger. She looked around the room, hoping to see the air shimmering somewhere. She wanted Louise-Anne to be there for this moment. There was no sign of her. Abi couldn't be sure what would be inside the box, but it just seemed right that Louise-Anne should be there to hear it. It would be better that way, rather than having to explain it to her bit by bit. It was her history, after all.

'This is a love story,' Abi began and all the boys groaned loudly, 'and a mystery,' she added quickly.

'Good,' muttered Jack.

'It involves HENRY GRAINGER,' she shouted, making them all jump, 'and LOUISE-ANNE MILLER.' She paused, waiting.

'Does this lecture come with volume control?' Chrissy demanded, and there were a few giggles.

'Sorry,' said Abi. 'I just wanted to be sure you all remember that name – LOUISE-ANNE MILLER,' she roared.

Apart from Sarah, Hannah, Grace and Simone, everyone else in the room was staring at her as if she'd just landed from outer space. Sarah bit her lip and looked around anxiously. Abi knew she must be wondering if this was the right way to break it to Louise-Anne that her father had been the cause of her misery. She had wondered herself what would happen when the ghost heard about her father's letter and the ring. It could be a complete disaster – but Louise-Anne had a right to know.

'Abi, speak normally, please,' Miss Flood warned.

'Yes, Miss,' Abi said, blushing. 'It's just important to remember that GRAINGER and MILLER are the key names in this story.'

'I think one of the others can do this bit, Abi,' Miss Flood said sharply. 'For some reason, you appear incapable of taking it seriously.'

Abi felt so foolish, but she wanted Louise-Anne to hear the names and put in an appearance. Just then, she saw Hannah give a little nod towards the hidden door of the writing room. She glanced over and, sure enough, the air was shimmering in that corner. Suddenly, Louise-Anne was there, watching them with curiosity. Abi took a deep breath. *Here goes nothing*, she thought.

'Sorry, Miss,' she said in her normal voice, 'just nerves. I'm ready to do it properly now.'

Abi gave a quick, reassuring smile to Louise-Anne, then began to tell the story of Henry Grainger and the wedding that never happened in 1886. When she came to the part about the records room in the gate lodge and the vault, the volunteers were leaning towards her, utterly hooked by what they were hearing.

'You went down into a vault *under* the gate lodge?' Jack asked, his eyes wide. 'Can I go and have a look?' he said pleadingly to Mr Grainger, who shook his head.

'It's not for public viewing,' Mr Grainger said

gently. 'The girls were there with good reason.' Jack looked very put out.

Abi glanced over to where Louise-Anne stood, motionless. She noticed that Grace had quietly left her seat and was standing next to the ghost, as if to comfort her. Abi could see that their arms were almost touching, and the air between them shimmered. It seemed to be working, though, as Louise-Anne was very calm. *She really wants to hear this*, Abi thought.

'Along with that letter,' Abi said, 'there was a book of Shakespeare's sonnets –' Mr Grainger held it up and she saw Louise-Anne give a jolt of recognition – 'and . . . this ring.' Mr Grainger held the ring up between his finger and thumb. Now Abi looked directly at Louise-Anne. 'It's a double ring – two wedding rings welded together. It arrived the day Louise-Anne Miller died, and we can only imagine that it was Henry's way of telling her that he still loved her.'

Louise-Anne moved closer, her eyes fixed unblinkingly on the double ring. She raised her hand, as if to touch it.

Watching Abi and her friends, a flash of understanding passed over Simone's face. She whispered in Sarah's ear, 'Is she here?'

Sarah nodded wordlessly, transfixed by the ghost whose face was showing a range of different emotions, from anger to love. When Abi spoke of the letter, Louise-Anne looked shocked, then angry, but now her face was soft with love and sorrow as she finally saw Henry's small symbol of his love for her. 'Poor Louise-Anne,' Grace breathed, holding back tears. Simone watched, fascinated, as the four girls all looked towards the same point in the room, watching the ghost they were trying to help.

'That's as far as we've gotten,' Abi finished, 'until now.' She returned to her seat beside her friends and took Sarah's hand in hers. 'I know you didn't want her to know about the letter, but I felt it was the right thing to do,' she whispered to her friend.

Sarah squeezed her hand. 'It's OK. It was the best way.'

Mr Grainger lifted Henry's deposit box in front of him. Louise-Anne moved closer to the table. Grace returned to her seat and the four girls waited to hear the final part of the ghost's story.

'This is the deposit box Henry Grainger took out in Louise-Anne Miller's name,' Mr Grainger said, as he slid the lid gently from the top of the box. Miss Flood was practically on her feet, straining to see what was inside. Very slowly and carefully, Mr Grainger lifted out . . . a small cylinder-shaped object.

'Is that it?' Sarah said, disappointed.

Mr Grainger smiled as he watched realization flood across Grace's face.

'Oh! Wow!' Grace said.

'Wow? Wow what?' Jack said impatiently. 'What is it, Grace?'

Grace stared at the object. 'Wow' was still all she could manage to say.

'*What is it?*' howled Jack and Sarah at the same time.

'It's a celluloid cylinder for an Edison phonograph,' Grace said. 'It's a . . . recording.'

They all stared at each other in disbelief. 'No way,' said Jack. 'A recording from, like, a hundred years ago?'

'But that's not possible, is it?' said Solomon.

'Yes, it is,' Grace said, nodding furiously. 'Henry had a phonograph – I saw it on the first day we came in here.'

'Henry was known for his interest in new inventions,' Mr Grainger said. 'He invested in a phonograph in the early years of their production. And this,' he said, holding up the wax cylinder, 'is *possibly*, as Grace said, a recording. What we need to do now is insert it into the machine and see if it actually works.'

'I put the phonograph in the sitting room,' Grace said breathlessly. 'Come on!'

The girls and their fellow volunteers all hurried across the hallway to the sitting room, with Mr Grainger following last, cradling his precious bundle. Louise-Anne was already in the sitting room when the girls entered, standing right next to the phonograph. She watched Mr Grainger intently as he gently inserted the cylinder into the wooden box at the base of the machine.

There was a silence, then a scratching sound as the mechanism whirred into motion. *Please let it work, please let it work*, Abi thought, her head bowed and her hands covering her eyes.

'*I . . . am Henry Grainger.*'

'Oh my goodness!' yelped Abi. She looked around wildly at her friends. 'It's *him*.' They were all staring in disbelief at the phonograph. Miss Flood looked as if someone had just told her she'd won a million pounds. Even Mr Grainger was staring at the old machine in shock. There was such a commotion of reaction that they missed what the voice was saying. Mr Grainger held up his hand.

'Please, we'll have to be very quiet to hear this,' he said, resetting the cylinder. 'I know it's overwhelming, but please stay quiet for the whole lot.'

The girls nudged each other and nodded towards Louise-Anne – she was standing over the phonograph, looking at it as if it might actually deliver her long-lost love into her arms.

'I hope this isn't going to upset her,' Hannah whispered anxiously. It was too late now. There was nothing on heaven or earth that could have moved Louise-Anne away from the source of that voice. Mr Grainger gestured for quiet and started the machine again.

'*I am Henry Grainger. I was betrothed to Louise-Anne Miller, whom I loved with all my heart. On the night we planned to marry, the thirty-first of October 1886, my brother came to me weeping, fearful for his life. He had compromised the honour of a young lady of our aunt's acquaintance and her father, an old-fashioned army gent, had demanded he marry her. When my brother refused, he challenged him to a duel. Charles was not familiar with pistols and Major Dillings –*'

The girls gasped at his name. 'Emilia's father,' Hannah whispered.

'*– was a crack shot, so my brother was in danger of losing his life. The duel was set for five of the morning and I accompanied him. The Major was very serious about his course of action. He had his man there to act as his second and he produced a box of duelling pistols and the* Code Duello, *which he read to us to apprise us of the received procedure. My brother pleaded with him, but to no avail. Indeed, his pleading seemed to make the man more determined to punish him. Charles prevailed upon me to take his place, saying our mother would be utterly distraught to be bereft of her youngest son. This was no doubt true. I offered this to the Major, but he refused and berated Charles for his cowardice.*

'*I could not stand by while any person deemed the Graingers cowards. I insisted I should duel in my brother's place, but again he declined and, furthermore, laughed at us. I urged Charles to gather his wits and face him like a man, for his own honour and our family's, but Charles continued to behave like a wretch, pleading with me to save him. All the while, the moon was slipping from the sky and I knew my love, my Louise-Anne, would be waiting for me. As I argued with my brother, the Major approached us again. He said that while he would not allow me to fight for my brother, he would allow me to preserve my family's name by marrying for him. I cannot describe the cold shock that gripped my heart at his words. I told him I was promised to marry that very morning, but he cared not. Charles, in a moment of pure selfishness, seized this moment of distraction to run from that place, mount his horse and ride off. I could not believe my eyes as I watched the clouds sent up by his horse's hooves. I turned to face the Major, and he was red in the face with unbridled anger. Striding towards his horse, he swore an oath and said he would go directly to my parents and tell them the truth about their son – and his ungentlemanly behaviour with the young lady. In that moment, facing the ruination of my brother and the ridicule of my family, I felt I could do nothing but accept the Major's offer and, by doing so, absolve my brother and protect my family. I said –'* there was the sound of a sharp intake of breath, as if Henry were trying not to cry – *'that I would go with him and in the place of my brother . . . marry his daughter.'*

There was a pause as Henry composed himself.
'I must live with my choice. I do not know what the

world holds, now or in the future, so I want to say the truth here and perhaps it will somehow reach her: Louise-Anne, I love you and only you. The rest is a deception and a wretched lie. I will go to my grave without loving Emilia, without producing any heirs to this grief that is my life. You, Louise-Anne, are my only love.

'*I have but one consolation. After your death, my sweet girl, I made a pact with your father to have your body delivered to me and an empty coffin placed in your grave in the cemetery. Under the cloak of night, I brought you myself to the mausoleum and interred you there, in the space where my own coffin will soon lie. We will be together in eternity, Louise-Anne, my love.*'

No one spoke. No one moved. The voice of Henry Grainger had seeped into the very walls and filled the house with a terrible sorrow. His voice shook with the grief of a man forced to live a lie. It was heartbreaking to hear him speak of the love he had denied himself, all for the honour of his family and his spineless brother.

The girls stared at Louise-Anne. She looked as if she had been turned to stone by the words she had just heard. Then, slowly, she turned round to face the four girls. Her face softened, and a smile spread across her lips and into the depths of her eyes. She looked beautiful. She glided across the room and came to rest beside them, her face seeming to glow from within. She stayed there, beside them, in silence, lost in her own feelings.

'Well,' said Miss Flood, falling back into her chair, 'that is simply extraordinary.' She looked at Abi, Grace, Hannah and Sarah and, without knowing, straight at Louise-Anne, too. 'I don't know what to say, girls,' she said, shaking her head, 'you've uncovered an incredible story.'

'Now I know why the grave was empty when that fellow took his soundings,' Mr Grainger said, smiling to himself.

'And now we know why there are thirteen burials in the mausoleum,' Grace said. 'The extra coffin is Louise-Anne's. Henry never told anyone it was there.'

'So that's why he didn't get to the church,' Hannah said slowly. 'He must have sent the messenger with the letter to explain to Louise-Anne what had happened, and that's the letter her father tore up. How must he have felt, following the Major in the opposite direction, to go and marry a girl he'd never even met?'

'And that's why the handwriting was different, too,' Abi said, 'because the letter, the fake letter, was written by the messenger.'

'I'd have let his brother face the firing squad,' Sarah said stoutly. 'He wasn't worth protecting.'

'You know what they say about blood being thicker than water,' Miss Flood said.

Everyone fell quiet again, unable to quite take in what they had just heard. Miss Flood went up to talk to Mr Grainger and the other kids followed, everyone crowding round to get a look at the machine and the cylinder while Mr Grainger showed them how it worked. The girls saw their chance.

'Writing room,' Abi whispered out of the corner of her mouth and the air shimmered and Louise-Anne was gone. One by one, they quietly left the room and headed for the drawing room.

'You have to come too,' Grace whispered to Simone, who smiled gratefully at her.

'I'd love to,' she whispered back and they slipped out and across the hallway.

They closed the drawing-room door tightly, then ran to open the hidden door. Simone was amazed to see the wall pop open to reveal the little room beyond. She hadn't known about it at all. They went inside, letting the door fall shut behind them. Louise-Anne was there, sitting on the stool at the bureau. She seemed bathed in a warm light and they couldn't take their eyes off her. Only Simone couldn't see the vision that lit up the room. She stood in the very corner, keeping out of the way.

'My friends,' Louise-Anne said happily, 'thank you so very much. You have returned my Henry to me. Now I know that he truly did love me, I can be at peace. At last.'

'But . . . what about your father?' Sarah said quietly.

Louise-Anne looked at her and her smile was touched with sadness. 'I forgive him,' she said simply. 'He did steal from me the knowledge of Henry's love, but Henry was already stolen from me by then. My father was wrong, but he loved me no less for it. I couldn't exist hating him – he's my father.'

Abi was delighted that they had uncovered the story of the thirteen burials. 'That's why we saw you in the mausoleum first,' she said, 'because you are connected to it, even if you didn't understand it yourself.'

Louise-Anne gave a feathery laugh. 'Yes, I have been searching for Henry all this time, and he was right there with me all along.' She shook her head, hardly able to believe all that had happened. She looked up at the girls again. 'It's time for me to go now,' she said gently. 'You have helped me, and I am eternally grateful.'

'We're glad we met you . . . and helped you,' Abi said, smiling. 'It's been some adventure.'

'I'll take my leave now,' Louise-Anne said. She raised her head and gave them a small wave, then the air started to shimmer all around her. She was gone.

'We did it,' Hannah said, her eyes shining with tears. 'We gave her the answer and now she's happy.'

'It looks to me like you're fully fledged ghost detectives now,' Simone remarked.

'Seriously?' groaned Sarah. 'You don't think we'll actually have to go through all that again, do you?'

'Don't you feel good to see Louise-Anne so happy?' Abi asked. 'I know I do.'

'Great, then you can deal with the next crazy ghost that turns up,' Sarah said, crossing her arms firmly. 'I'm hanging up my ghost detective hat and retiring.'

'What about this place?' Simone said, looking around the secret writing room. 'Are you going to show it to Miss Flood now?'

The girls looked at each other and slowly shook their heads. 'No,' said Hannah, 'it's Beryl's room, isn't it? No need to have everyone traipsing through it.' They nodded in silent agreement and Simone smiled gratefully.

'Come on,' said Grace, 'let's go back before they come looking for us. I've had a great idea to put to Miss Flood.' They all looked at her. She grinned. 'We're going to blow their socks off on the opening night with our incredible exhibit . . . *The Thirteenth Body in the Mausoleum*!'

17

The Museum

'*Now!*'

At Miss Flood's call, all the volunteers struck their matches and lit the wicks inside the pumpkin heads. Josh flipped the main switch. The volunteers ran to join together in a single group in front of the house, standing in silence, waiting. Suddenly, the darkness was punctured by hundreds of small lights. Dotted among them, nearer the house, were the larger lights of hanging lanterns. On the ground along the front of the house, ten pumpkins lit garishly from within added to the effect. It looked magical.

It was Hallowe'en night, just forty-five minutes before their launch party was due to start. They had been there since lunchtime and had spent hours twining fairy lights around the trees, setting up lanterns and cutting faces into pumpkins.

Abi was enchanted by the effect of the lights. 'That's so amazing,' she breathed, eyes wide in delight.

'It looks brilliant,' Jack said, laughing. 'We really did a good job!'

'Look over there,' Solomon said, pointing at the trees, 'I even put lights round one of the creatures. I hope he doesn't object!'

They grinned and clapped each other on the back, bowled over by the scene they had created.

They hadn't been sure if it would look as good as they hoped, but standing there in front of their museum, seeing the lights leading the way in for their visitors, they all felt really proud of themselves.

Abi stood in silence, thinking back to the moment she had first signed up to this project. It had been so worth it. She looked over at Hannah, Grace and Sarah. It was their friendship that she would treasure most out of all this – it meant everything to her – but, on top of that, they'd managed to get all the work done and make the house look magical. She smiled to herself in delight. She was so thankful that she had decided to volunteer. She would never forget this moment.

The door to the museum was standing open and the light glowed out from the reception area. Inside, the reception desk was neatly stacked with information sheets, the hooks on the wall waiting for visitors' coats to be hung there. In every room, the wooden furniture was polished to a high shine, the exhibits were set out perfectly, the explanation cards were waiting to be read and the soundtrack

183

was ready, at the press of a button, to deliver a real 'living history' feel to the whole show. The volunteers had worked so hard, for so many weeks – but now, every minute was worth it.

'Well done, everyone,' Miss Flood said, beaming at them. 'It's beyond what I even thought possible.'

'We've haven't got long before everyone arrives,' Grace said, 'so come on, let me show you the uniforms.'

They all went back into the house and Grace ran to the large bag she had brought and pulled out a stack of T-shirts. There was one for every volunteer, and she handed them round. They unfurled them and Abi smiled. 'Wow, these are so you, Grace. I love it!'

The T-shirts were red, and in bright yellow on the front, across the chest, was the word HELPER. On the back in the same acid yellow it said: ASK ME IF YOU NEED HELP!

'They're cool, Grace,' Jack said.

Grace blushed and shrugged off the compliment. 'Ah, it's just so people can find us in the crowds.'

'I wouldn't say *cool* exactly,' Elaine muttered under her breath, and Chrissy sniggered.

'I have one more,' Grace said, reaching into the bag again. She drew out another red T-shirt. 'This is for you, Miss,' she said, handing it to Miss Flood.

'Me?' said Miss Flood, surprised. She unfurled her T-shirt and they all burst out laughing. On the front it read: THE BOSS. On the back: DON'T BOTHER ME!

'Grace Quinn!' Miss Flood said, then she laughed loudly. 'I think I'll wear this at home!' she joked. 'Right then,' she went on briskly, 'we have our uniforms, we have the place ready, I think we're just about ready for a grand opening!'

For the last time, they went together from room to room, checking everything. The museum looked wonderful. The bedrooms, study and schoolroom were all set up as if the family had just left a moment before. There was a rope across the stairs leading to the attic rooms, as they weren't opening to the public. Downstairs in the kitchen, every pot and pan gleamed and a fire was set in the grate of the massive fireplace, as if the housekeeper was on her way to light it. The tables were scrubbed down and there were ingredients on the big wooden table, as if the cook was about to set to work on an elaborate meal. The games room, gunroom, library, ballroom, sitting and drawing rooms – everywhere it looked like the family had just stepped outside for a moment, in the middle of enjoying their normal pastimes.

On the invitations sent out to the guests, Miss Flood had promised that there would be a 'Very Special Exhibit'. Hannah, Abi, Sarah and Grace had worked flat out on creating *The Thirteenth Body in the Mausoleum*. Abi couldn't wait to see what people would think of it. It started in the main house, then they would invite anyone who was interested to go down to the mausoleum to see the extra coffin for themselves. They had lit the path to the mausoleum with garden candles, and it looked so exciting.

'OK,' said Miss Flood, as they returned down the staircase to the reception area. 'Just take a breather now so you're ready when they all start to arrive.'

'Seriously,' said Sarah, 'I feel like I've eaten too many sweets and can't sit still. I'm so nervous.'

'I know,' Grace groaned. 'This is the worst bit – waiting. I just want to get started now.'

'My head's a bit fuzzy,' Abi said, fanning her face with her hand. 'I think I need some air. I'm just going to walk outside for a few minutes.'

She headed out through the front door and walked into the cold darkness. She looked back at the house and thought that it looked like a cross between a haunted house and a magical fairy castle. As she stood there, taking it all in, someone walked quickly out of the house and down the drive towards her. It was Josh. He walked straight over to her.

'Hi, Abi,' he said, 'do you have a minute?'

Abi felt her heart skip a beat: what did Josh want? 'Sure,' she said.

'Walk over here,' he said, 'away from the house. I want to show you something.'

Abi glanced around, but everyone else was inside – there was no one but her and Josh. She followed him, stumbling over the dark path, until he came to a halt on the grass beyond the gravel driveway. 'Come over here,' he said. She stood beside him, gazing out on the darkness of the parkland that stretched out in front of the house. 'I had an idea,' Josh said, 'but I didn't run it by Miss Flood. I need you to take a look and tell me if it's any good or not.'

Abi squinted out into the darkness, wondering what he had done. 'Where is it?' she asked.

'Turn around,' he said softly.

She turned to face the house. 'And . . . what am I looking at?' she said.

'Look up,' he said. 'At the top windows.'

Abi craned her head back and looked at the full front of the house. 'Oh, wow. Josh, that looks fantastic,' she breathed.

'Really?' he said. 'It's not a stupid idea?'

On the ground in front of the house, the pumpkin faces leered in the candle flames lighting them from within, and the lights blazed in the ground- and first-floor rooms of the house. Normally, the attic windows were dark and blank, but Josh had gone up there and hung orange paper in each window, covering all of the glass, then put on the lights in the rooms. The effect was wonderful – the windows glowed orange, making the house look like it was celebrating Hallowe'en in its own way. It was perfect. The house was, after all, practically one of them after everything the volunteers had done. It had its own unique character.

'No, that's not a stupid idea at all,' Abi said, smiling at him. 'It's brilliant.' She felt like pinching herself – she couldn't believe that the moody, unreachable Josh Fitzsimons was standing here, asking her opinion like this. It seemed so unlike him.

Without warning, Josh suddenly grabbed Abi's hand and put a finger over his lips, indicating for her to stay quiet. Abi's skin tingled where Josh held her hand and she didn't know where to look. He tugged gently at her hand, taking a step backwards into the darkness, gesturing for Abi to follow him. They crept further and further, step by step, into the darkness beyond the lights until it cloaked them, making them invisible.

Abi didn't think she'd breathed for two whole minutes by now. Was this it? Was she about to have her very first kiss?

Josh leant closer, then suddenly he turned and whispered in her ear a word that sounded like . . . kissy? That wasn't exactly the romantic way she thought this might go.

'Excuse me?' Abi asked, flustered. 'Er, no, I don't think kissy . . . I mean, kissing, is a good idea actually, but . . .'

'*Shhhh*, no!' Josh looked at her in amusement and then pointed at the driveway. 'Look,' he whispered.

She looked and saw Chrissy and Elaine making their way through the shadows, not far from where she and Josh stood.

'Chrissy,' Josh whispered again, nodding in their direction.

'Oh . . . right, Chrissy,' Abi whispered quickly, wishing the ground would open and swallow her up – right now!

Josh leant close again and whispered in her ear, 'They can't see us. Don't move. What are they doing?'

Abi tried to steady her breathing as she looked at the two girls, who were scuttling through the darkness like thieves. She squinted at them, then realized they were carrying something between them. She could make out a hat and wild hair. It looked like they were carrying some sort of doll. What could they be up to?

'Hold up your end properly, Elaine,' Chrissy hissed loudly. 'And go faster, before anyone sees us. Come on!'

They hurried across the grass, passing a few metres from Josh and Abi, then kept going towards the side wall, then around and into the back of the house. Once they had passed out of sight, Josh looked at Abi. 'What was that thing they were carrying?' he said.

'It looked like a doll or something,' Abi said. 'I've no idea what they're doing with it. It's not part of any exhibit that I know.'

Josh frowned. 'I wouldn't trust either of them,' he said darkly. 'Come on, let's follow them and see where they're going.'

Abi gathered herself, trying to get over the embarrassment of what had just not happened.

'Are you coming?' whispered Josh.

'Yes, right behind you,' Abi said, pushing all thoughts of Josh and his hand in hers out of her mind. She raced after him, towards the side wall. They moved as quickly and quietly as they could. When they reached the wall, Josh went first to check where Chrissy and Elaine were. He motioned to Abi to come and join him, and they ran across the back courtyard and through the archway in the hedge wall beyond. Now they were on the path that led around the perimeter of the garden.

'Which way?' Abi said, looking in both directions.

'Listen,' said Josh. They listened and, sure enough, they could hear the girls heading in the direction of the maze, still arguing about who was carrying the heaviest end.

'Let's catch up, but be really quiet,' Josh whispered.

'This is great,' Abi whispered back, eyes shining, 'I feel like I'm in a Nancy Drew book!' Josh smiled at her. 'Look at me talking books,' she said, blushing. 'Hannah would be so proud!'

They headed off in the same direction as the two girls, moving as silently as possible. They trailed after them as Chrissy and Elaine went past the Lovers' Arbour, past the labyrinth and on past the pet cemetery. When they reached the mausoleum, they stopped and put down the thing they had been carrying. Josh and Abi slipped through the darkness and hid behind a tree growing next to the mausoleum, waiting to see what would happen next.

'That thing is so heavy,' Elaine whined, 'and I've got blisters on my hands now.'

'Well, you were the one who said it had to be a scarecrow,' Chrissy snapped. 'I just wanted a scary mask on the door, but you were the one who said a witch scarecrow would be better.'

Elaine grinned. 'But wasn't I right?' she said, propping up the scarecrow. 'It looks so scary. It's going to be brilliant.'

'Yeah, you were right,' Chrissy said with a laugh. 'That thing is horrible.'

'What are they up to?' Abi whispered. Josh and Abi strained to see the 'scarecrow'. It was made of two poles tied together with a bit of rope, to make a cross-shaped body. They had put a long black cloak around it – like the ones kids wore when they dressed up as wizards. On top was a really ugly witch mask with straggly hair, and a pointy witch's hat glued on top. It was only home-made, but in the half-light from the garden candles, and standing next to the mausoleum, it looked pretty scary. If you didn't know what it was, it would definitely give you a fright.

'This is going to be so good,' Chrissy said. 'The Nerd Herd think their stupid exhibit is the best thing here. An extra body in a coffin – so what? Only those girls could think that was interesting.'

'I know,' Elaine said. 'They'd be better off getting a manicure and a decent hairdo than hanging out in graveyards counting coffins!'

The two girls laughed nastily – or, as Abi thought to herself, cackled just like witches. She could not believe what she was hearing. She would never have thought that Chrissy and Elaine would go this far, to actually try to ruin the exhibit. Okay, they had been truly horrible to Sarah, but she still didn't think they disliked her and her friends *that* much. But they had gone to so much trouble to make the witch. It was incredible.

'OK,' said Chrissy, looking at her watch. 'We have to be quick. Do you think we'll put it inside or outside?'

'Um, how about in the doorway?' Elaine said. 'When Miss Flood shines her torch on it, it will look so awful.'

'I don't know,' Chrissy said, 'I was thinking

maybe outside the door, so they can see it as they come up the path and are wondering what it is. It'll make them nervous first, then they'll get a real fright when they see it up close.'

'But what if —' Elaine began, but then stopped short. She looked around. 'Did you hear something?' she said.

'No,' Chrissy said, sounding impatient. 'Now focus, Elaine, come on. How are we going to do this?'

Abi clamped her hand over her mouth, trying not to laugh as Josh once again rubbed together the two brittle branches he had picked up to make a *crrr-crrr* sound. He was going to turn the tables on the two girls!

This time, Chrissy looked up and glanced towards the trees.

'You did hear it, too,' Elaine said accusingly. 'I told you there was something.'

'It's just . . . nothing,' Chrissy said, trying to sound sure of herself. 'Come on, let's just put it up at the door here and get back to the house.'

They began to drag the witch into place in front of the mausoleum. A garden candle nearby cracked and spat, and they both jumped. They were definitely spooked now. Josh bent low and scooted around to a different tree and rubbed the branches together again, louder this time. From her hiding place Abi joined in, making a scratching sound by pulling a twig down the bark of the tree. She crouched down again, out of sight.

Chrissy and Elaine backed into each other, looking all around.

'I don't like this,' Elaine whimpered. 'I can definitely hear something, Chrissy, out there in the trees.'

'Do you think anyone saw us up at the house?' Chrissy asked suspiciously. 'Maybe *someone* is hiding there making noises,' she shouted in the direction of Abi's tree. 'Maybe *someone* is trying to scare us. If you're there, you'd better come out now,' she said bravely, 'or I'm coming in to find you.'

Shoot! thought Abi. She couldn't see Josh any more, but she could hear the sticks rubbing again – he was trying to draw the girls' attention away. But Chrissy had taken a step forward now – another few steps and she'd walk straight on top of Abi. She bit her lip, wondering what to do. *Hang on*, she thought suddenly. *They're in the wrong here. I'm just going to step out and tell them exactly what I think of . . .*

Before she could move, she was stopped by a scream from Elaine.

'What? What is it?' Chrissy demanded.

'Something . . . something touched my arm,' Elaine wailed. 'It was so cold.'

'Pull it together,' Chrissy hissed, 'you're just imagining things, you idiot!'

How did Josh manage to do that? Abi thought. *Pretty impressive!*

Suddenly, another scream came from the clearing. This time it was Chrissy. 'I felt it! I felt it!' she yelled. 'It touched my cheek.'

Elaine started crying, grabbing Chrissy's hand and holding it tight. 'There it is again!' she howled. 'Get away from me!'

The two girls began batting at the air around them, lashing out at nothing. From their hiding places, Abi and Josh stared in bewilderment as Chrissy and Elaine acted as if they were being attacked by an invisible swarm of wasps. What was going on? Elaine flung the witch to the ground and, clutching hands tightly, the two girls ran for the path, racing through the trees and disappearing out of sight.

Josh stepped out from behind his tree and looked at Abi in confusion. 'What happened there?' he said.

'I don't know,' Abi said, shaking her head. But just as she spoke, she noticed a patch of air in the clearing shimmering. She smiled. She felt a cold wisp of air brush past her, gently. 'Thank you, Louise-Anne,' she whispered with a grin.

Josh walked into the clearing and picked up the girls' scarecrow witch. He looked at it and shuddered. 'That is a freaky thing, isn't it?' he said, holding it out to show Abi.

'I just can't believe they went to all that trouble,' Abi said. 'Like, how much do they hate us?'

Josh shrugged. 'I've no idea what goes on in Chrissy's head,' he said, 'but she's never liked anyone doing better than her. Anyway, we'd better get this thing out of sight and get back to the house.'

'The launch party!' Abi said, realizing how long they'd been gone.

Josh held out his hand and Abi blushed as she realized that this time he didn't need to, he was doing it because he wanted to. She took it shyly.

Josh smiled at her. 'Come on!'

18

The Thirteenth Body in the Mausoleum

Abi and Josh burst through the door into the reception area, panting from running so hard. Their friends crowded round them.

'Where were you?' Jack asked. 'It's almost eight.'

'Just had a final job to see to,' Josh said, winking at Abi. She could see Hannah, Grace and Sarah staring at her, open-mouthed – she'd have some explaining to do!

'Are Chrissy and Elaine here?' Josh asked.

'Yeah, they ran in a few minutes ago,' Jack said. 'They looked freaked. I think they went for a walk in the back garden and scared themselves silly. Elaine was going on about something cold on her arm. I've no idea what she was talking about.'

Abi and Josh looked at each and grinned.

'What's going on?' Daniel asked, catching the look that passed between them.

'Chrissy and Elaine had a plan to scare anyone

visiting the mausoleum tonight,' Josh said. 'Let's just say we aborted the mission,' he added, unable to stop laughing now.

Just then, Chrissy and Elaine walked in, still holding hands. When they saw the rest of the volunteers laughing, they looked at them angrily.

'What are you all laughing at?' Chrissy demanded.

'Has something put you in a bad mood?' Josh said innocently, but with a wicked grin.

Chrissy stared at him for a few moments, then she blushed fiercely. 'It was *you*!' she said.

'Yes, it was,' Josh said. 'And you should be thanking me, both of you, because I just saved you from getting into serious trouble with Miss Flood. If you had freaked out the guests, she would have thrown you out of here.'

Chrissy looked like she was going to explode with anger; she was shaking, her lips pressed tightly together.

'I don't believe it,' Elaine said weakly. 'But how did you *do* that?'

'That's none of your business,' Josh said. 'It was so bad, what you did, trying to ruin the girls' exhibit. We've all worked so hard for tonight.'

Grace, Hannah and Sarah crowded round Abi. 'What happened? Tell us, go on,' they pleaded.

'Later,' Abi whispered. 'I'll tell you the whole story.'

Before Chrissy could say anything more, Miss

Flood clapped her hands. 'Places, everyone,' she called. 'The first guests are about to come through the door!'

The volunteers, all wearing their red-and-yellow T-shirts, lined up in a row in front of the reception desk. They forgot about Chrissy and her silly prank as they greeted people and watched their delight at seeing the new, revamped museum. Their parents were among the first to arrive, smiling widely at them and giving the thumbs-up – proud that their children had been the ones to do this project. Sarah's mother and brother, Aaron, came in together, and Abi saw a look of disappointment on her friend's face as she realized her father wasn't with them. She went over and gave Sarah a quick hug.

After that, things got really busy and none of them could focus on anything but the job in hand. A stream of people from the town arrived, including a journalist and photographer from the local newspaper. The photographer took a few shots of the line of volunteers, and asked for their names. Then the volunteers had to greet people as they arrived, hang up coats, direct them round the exhibits and hand out refreshments. Chrissy and Elaine looked sullen and angry the whole time; Abi and Josh exchanged shy smiles whenever they passed each other.

Sarah and Grace were standing at the reception

desk when Miss Belsham from the records office came through the front door. She was dressed for a night out, in a glittery dress with a purple feather boa slung over her shoulders. Sarah stared, but Grace immediately went up to her. 'You look fabulous,' she said. 'You are rocking that feather boa!'

Miss Belsham smiled at her. 'I hear you solved the mystery about Henry Grainger,' she said. 'I can't wait to hear about it. I'm so jealous you uncovered it.'

'I promise it's worth waiting for,' Grace said.

Miss Belsham headed off to chat to some friends as Abi and Hannah came up to join the girls at the reception desk.

'That's the third tour I've given already,' Abi said. 'I'm pooped and it's still early!'

'Hello there,' Mr Grainger's voice called out. 'Got room for two more?' He stepped into the reception area with Simone beside him, both looking around in delight.

'Welcome, welcome,' Abi called. 'It's so good to see you.'

'This is incredible,' Simone said. 'I can't believe so many people have turned out.'

'I know,' said Grace. 'The place is crammed. Make sure you get to your spot in our exhibit in good time – we'll be opening it once the mayor gets here.'

'Will do,' said Mr Grainger, beaming at them. 'And well done, all of you. I can tell you, my parents would be very proud to see this night.'

As he wandered off towards the stairs, Simone raised an eyebrow and said mischievously, 'And are my grandparents here to see this night?'

The girls laughed and Sarah punched her playfully on the arm. 'No, it's all clear since Louise-Anne left,' she said. 'We're a ghost-free zone, and hopefully we'll stay that way!'

Simone smiled at them from under her thick black fringe. 'Love the T-shirts, by the way,' she said, and Grace grinned happily.

There was a sudden burst of activity at the front door and Miss Flood called out excitedly, 'The mayor is here!'

'She couldn't be more excited if the president himself was coming to have a look,' Sarah muttered under her breath, making her friends giggle. The other volunteers gathered quickly and once again the ten of them lined up in the reception area. There was a flash from the photographer's camera as a small, brightly smiling woman came in. A man in a smart suit stepped in and stood close beside her.

'Which one is your mayor?' Abi whispered out of the corner of her mouth.

'The one with the major necklace bling,' Sarah whispered back.

'I didn't know the mayor was a woman!' Abi said, surprised.

'Mrs Lowe, Mayor,' Miss Flood said, almost bowing, 'we are so honoured to have you here tonight.'

'I'm very much looking forward to it,' the mayor replied cheerfully. 'The drive up was certainly spectacular, with all those lights.'

The mayor was given the grand tour, with the rest of the visitors trailing behind her. As she walked into each room, Daniel and Josh activated the audio for the first time, and everyone was amazed by how good it was. In the sitting room there were sounds of polite, subdued conversation, the soft clinking of china teacups and the sound of classical music; in the kitchen it was loud and raucous, with instructions being bellowed, pots clattering and water whooshing down Belfast sinks; in the schoolroom, children's voices intoned their Latin verbs; and in the ballroom a waltz swooned through the room and there was the sound of feet dancing. It was simply brilliant, and the journalist scribbled notes as he went around behind the mayor, taking it all in.

Finally, they came back to the ground floor, and Miss Flood announced that they would now view the Very Special Exhibit: *The Thirteenth Body in the Mausoleum*. A hum of excitement spread through the crowd – most people had heard that the volunteers had discovered an interesting story, but no one knew exactly what it was. Miss Flood led the mayor and the guests to the drawing room, where the girls had set up the introduction to the exhibit.

'I am very pleased to announce tonight,' their teacher began, 'that during our preparations, four of our young volunteers discovered and followed up a fascinating story concerning one member of the Grainger family, Henry Grainger. Born in 1868, Henry married Emilia Dillings of Templeton in 1886, but Abi, Grace, Sarah and Hannah discovered that there was far more to the story than that. It transpired that Henry had been betrothed to a local girl, Louise-Anne Miller. On the night of their planned secret wedding, Henry failed to turn up. Why? Well, the answer to that question turned out to be tied into the fact that, as Grace noticed, there are *thirteen* burials in the Grainger family mausoleum, not twelve as all the records show.'

Everyone was listening intently to Miss Flood as she spoke. Hannah, Sarah, Abi and Grace looked at each other and smiled proudly.

'In fact,' she went on, 'the girls found out that Henry was forced to marry Emilia after a duel his brother refused to fight, in order to save his family's honour. Four days after he left his true love waiting at the altar, he married Emilia Dillings and settled into a sorrowful life in a loveless union. As for his jilted bride, she died of a fever two days after he failed to show up at the church. His only consolation was the fact that he had made a pact with Louise-Anne's father to spirit her body away and bury it secretly in the mausoleum. That is why there is a thirteenth coffin – an extra body in the mausoleum, which has only been discovered and explained now, by my four fantastic students!'

An excited murmur ran through the crowd as the extraordinary events of Henry and Louise-Anne's love story were described. The visitors moved about among the exhibits the girls had set up: the book of Shakespeare's sonnets inscribed by Henry, the double-ring displayed on a black velvet cushion, the letter of confession by Mr Miller, which was displayed face-up in a glass cabinet. There was also the list of the burials in the mausoleum, given to them by Miss Belsham, which was displayed alongside the book on the family, opened at the page declaring there to be twelve Grainger burials in the mausoleum. At the end of the room, in front of the window, stood the phonograph, with Mr Grainger standing guard beside it.

'Now,' said Miss Flood, 'I invite you all to listen to a unique and extraordinary recording unearthed by Mr Grainger in the vaults of Grainger Undertakers. This will not be played again because repeated use might damage the cylinder, so future visitors will only get to read a transcript of the recording. Tonight, however, you are privileged to be able to listen to the voice of . . . Henry Grainger.'

Miss Flood raised her arm towards the phonograph, like a magician about to pull a rabbit from a hat. Mr Grainger bent forward and set the machine in motion. The four girls grabbed each other's hands, unable to believe that their strange adventure had led to this moment, when the truth of Henry's love for Louise-Anne was at last spoken across the centuries.

'*I . . . am Henry Grainger . . .*'

After the recording finished, the crowd clapped loudly, with some people dabbing tears from their eyes.

'We will now conclude this extraordinary exhibit where it began,' Miss Flood said, 'in the mausoleum.'

Those who were willing to brave the cold pulled their coats tightly round themselves and headed for the back door. They trooped outside, led by Miss Flood with a torch. The visitors made their way along the path, curving their way towards the mausoleum. Once there, Miss Flood announced that she would let them in in groups of ten, ushering each group out after a few minutes, so that everyone could get a chance to see inside. The first group was Miss Flood, the mayor and her husband, the two Graingers, the four girls and Miss Belsham. They waited while the photographer set up the equipment to take a photo of them outside the mausoleum.

Simone joined the girls. 'Well done, it's amazing. Are you very excited?' she whispered.

'I've got butterflies in my tummy,' Grace said.

'Everyone loves it,' Simone said, smiling. 'You've really brought the place alive again,' she said. 'Thank you.'

'Chrissy almost brought the house down with a witch!' Abi whispered to them.

Simone and the other three girls looked at her, puzzled. 'What do you mean?' Sarah said. 'What happened down here?'

'I'll describe it all later,' Abi said. 'In monstrous detail!'

'Just make sure I'm there when you do,' Simone said, grinning.

'Now,' Miss Flood called. 'Are we ready?'

They stepped inside the mausoleum. The girls had set up candles to light up the interior and against the back wall, under the carving of the egg-timer, stood a mannequin, wearing a perfect copy of Louise-Anne's wedding dress. Grace had drawn it up, based on first-hand experience, of course, and her mother, who was really good at sewing and knitting, had helped her to make it. It looked eerily beautiful in the candlelight, as the visitors counted the coffins and urns, marvelling to find there were, in fact, thirteen.

'Where did you find the design for the dress?' the mayor asked, as she put on her glasses to examine it more closely. 'It's absolutely beautiful,' she said, 'and so authentic to the period.'

Grace winked at her friends as Miss Flood told the mayor how the girls had researched fashion history books to find the right design for the dress.

'You have a future in fashion, I think,' the mayor said to Grace. She was looking at Grace's pink Converse, the green skirt she had teamed with her red T-shirt and the big red rose she had twined into her hair. 'You look the part,' she said with a smile.

'Thank you, mayor,' Grace said. 'It was really hard to make the dress so quickly, but I did it with my mother. We worked every evening after school.'

'You must be pleased the exhibit has turned out so well?' the mayor said to Abi.

'Yes, ma'am,' Abi said.

'Oh, you're American,' the mayor said. 'And you've moved to the town?'

'Yes, just this summer,' Abi said. 'But I've already made some amazing friends,' she added, motioning to Grace, Sarah, Hannah and Simone.

'I'm glad to hear it,' the mayor said, smiling, 'and you're very welcome to our town. Aren't you lucky that the first thing you get involved in is one of the best things the town has ever seen?'

'I really am,' Abi said with a laugh. 'I could

never have even imagined this place, believe me!'

There was no doubt about it – the whole night had been a huge success, and the *Thirteenth Body* exhibit was the thing everyone was talking about. The photographer asked if he could take one more picture – of the four girls standing in the mausoleum, next to the wedding dress. They stood close together, smiling happily as the flash lit up the interior for a moment, before they were plunged into darkness again.

As the last visitor called their goodbyes and left through the front door, Miss Flood stood with the volunteers' parents, talking about how wonderful they all were. 'Well,' she said to them with a huge smile, 'that was a night *I'll* never forget!'

The volunteers stood together in a corner of the reception area, tired out but still smiling.

'We are heroes,' Jack said. 'The town loves us!'

'Don't let it go to your head,' Hannah said, laughing. 'We're not superheroes.'

'I think Daniel and Josh should take a bow,' Sarah said. 'The soundtrack really made it, didn't it?'

'Oh, come on,' Daniel said, 'everyone played their part. And look at you lot – toast of the town with your Henry Grainger stuff.'

The girls grinned at him. 'Just doin' our job,' Grace joked, tipping an imaginary hat.

Chrissy couldn't contain herself any longer. 'Stop acting like a bunch of dweebs,' she snapped at them. 'It's just a project. What do you sound like? So full of yourselves.'

'Come on, Chrissy,' Josh said, 'put another record on. You don't really want to keep going on like this, do you?'

Chrissy shot a dark look at him, then took a step towards him. 'I am going to get you back, Josh Fitzsimons, for what you did to me and Elaine.'

Abi stepped between them. 'There's no need to be like that, Chrissy,' she said firmly. 'You had a pretty nasty plan yourself, remember?'

Chrissy stared at her for a moment. 'Oh, so you were his little helper, were you? That makes sense,' she said, thinking how the noises she'd heard had come from two different places. 'Well then, I'm going to get you back too,' she said angrily, then marched off, leaving the volunteers staring after her.

'Elaine,' Abi said, 'please don't keep going along with her. Can't you get her to see she's just making life hard for herself? She nearly got you into deep trouble tonight.'

Elaine hesitated for a minute, but then her normal pout returned. 'Chrissy is just sick and tired of seeing you four taking all the credit,' she said. 'We *will* figure out a way to get you out of this museum, just you wait and see.' She turned and walked off after Chrissy.

'Can someone please tell the rest of us what that's all about?' Solomon begged. 'I'm dying to know what happened earlier.'

'They had a silly idea to scare people at the mausoleum,' Josh said. 'They made a witch scarecrow thing and were going to prop it up at the door.'

The others stared at him in shock. That really went beyond a prank – it was sabotage.

'And how did you stop them?' Daniel asked.

Before Josh could answer, a late arrival hurried over to them.

'Sarah?'

They all looked round, and there stood Sarah's father in a creased suit, his tie loosened. He looked tired.

'Sarah,' he repeated, 'I'm so sorry I'm late. Work . . .' He trailed off.

Sarah bit her lip and said nothing. Abi, Grace and Hannah exchanged a look as the others watched, wondering what was going on now. 'Hi, Dad,' Sarah said in a voice that didn't sound like her at all.

'I know you're all finishing up for the night,' he said, 'but I'd really love it if you'd show me round. I'd like to see what you've been doing.' He looked around the reception area. 'It really looks impressive.'

There was a silence as Sarah looked at her dad, then Josh spoke up. 'Hi, Mr Forde. Sarah, if you'd like to give your dad the tour, I'll make sure the audio is working in each room so he gets the full show.'

Abi smiled gratefully at Josh for his kindness to her friend. She couldn't believe how different he seemed now from the reserved boy she'd met on their first day as volunteers.

'OK, Dad,' Sarah said quietly. 'If you'd like to see it, I'll show you round.'

'Great,' her father said, looking relieved.

They headed off, and the other volunteers said goodnight and drifted off to gather their things and rejoin their parents. Abi, Hannah and Grace watched Sarah as she walked with her father up the main staircase.

'Do you think Sarah'll get her wish?' Abi asked.

'Wish?' Grace said with a frown. 'What wish?'

'That we won't ever have another adventure like that one,' Abi said.

'Oh, that,' said Hannah, smiling. 'I don't know.'

'I don't either,' said Grace thoughtfully. 'But it's hard to think that there could be any more ghosts knocking around this place, isn't it? Everything seems so . . . normal now. Like it was all just a dream.'

At that moment, the moon and stars became a little blurry as the night air over the town shimmered for a moment, before settling again. The lights twinkled along the driveway and the stone creatures stared out from their watching posts. Sarah and her father made their way towards the mausoleum, where Louise-Anne Miller slept peacefully next to her love, Henry Grainger. It seemed that something had shifted in the world, and couldn't be changed back.

Acknowledgements

There were a number of people who read the drafts of this book and gave me really helpful advice and opinions. For that, I would like to thank Aisling Rafferty – of Boston and Drogheda – whose enthusiasm for the characters and the story helped me enormously. Thank you, Aisling. Thanks also to 'reader-in-chief' Gayle Pierce, who was the perfect sounding board, even under pressure! Thank you to Adele McGuirk, who gave me astute feedback exactly when it was needed, and to Bernie and Hugh Conaghy for giving me the thumbs-up! Thank you to Faith O'Grady for her constant support.

The editors at Puffin have been a joy to work with, so thank you, Shannon Park, Lindsey Heaven, Wendy Shakespeare and Karen Whitlock. A very special thanks to Paddy O'Doherty, who championed this book from the start and was a generous, perceptive and intelligent editor. For all your help, Paddy, thank you.

And last but most: thank you, Donagh.

Bright and shiny and sizzling with fun stuff . . .

puffin.co.uk

WEB FUN

UNIQUE and exclusive digital content!
Podcasts, photos, Q&A, Day in the Life of, interviews
and much more, from Eoin Colfer, Cathy Cassidy,
Allan Ahlberg and Meg Rosoff to Lynley Dodd!

WEB NEWS

The **Puffin Blog** is packed with posts and photos from
Puffin HQ and special guest bloggers. You can also sign up
to our monthly newsletter **Puffin Beak Speak**

WEB CHAT

Discover something new EVERY month –
books, competitions and treats galore

WEBBED FEET

(Puffins have funny little feet and
brightly coloured beaks)

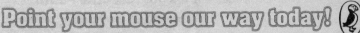

Point your mouse our way today!

It all started with a Scarecrow.

Puffin is seventy years old.
Sounds ancient, doesn't it? But Puffin has never been
so lively. We're always on the lookout for the next big
idea, which is how it began all those years ago.

Penguin Books was a big idea from the mind of
a man called Allen Lane, who in 1935 invented
the quality paperback and changed the world.
**And from great Penguins, great Puffins grew,
changing the face of children's books forever.**

The first four Puffin Picture Books were hatched in 1940 and the
first Puffin story book featured a man with broomstick arms called
Worzel Gummidge. In 1967 Kaye Webb, Puffin Editor, started the
Puffin Club, promising to **'make children into readers'**.
She kept that promise and over 200,000 children became
devoted Puffineers through their quarterly instalments of
Puffin Post, which is

Many years from no
remember Puffin with a
or what you're into,
The possibilities are
whether it's a picture
or a hardback, i
on it – it'